Sm~~~~ ~~~~
Hero

Small Town Hero

LINDA LAEL MILLER

MAISEY YATES

KENSINGTON
PUBLISHING CORP.

kensingtonbooks.com

KENSINGTON BOOKS are published by

Kensington Publishing Corp.
900 Third Avenue
New York, NY 10022

All Kensington titles, imprints, and distributed lines are available at special quantity discounts for bulk purchases for sales promotion, premiums, fund-raising, educational, or institutional use.

This book is a work of fiction. Names, characters, businesses, organizations, places, events, and incidents either are the product of the author's imagination or are used fictitiously. Any resemblance to actual persons, living or dead, events, or locales is entirely coincidental.

To the extent that the image or images on the cover of this book depict a person or persons, such person or persons are merely models, and are not intended to portray any character or characters featured in the book.

Special book excerpts or customized printings can also be created to fit specific needs. For details, write or phone the office of the Kensington Sales Manager: Kensington Publishing Corp., 900 Third Avenue, New York, NY 10022. Attn. Sales Department. Phone: 1-800-221-2647.

KENSINGTON and the K with book logo Reg. US Pat. & TM Off.

ISBN: 978-1-4967-5371-7 (ebook)
ISBN: 978-1-4967-5370-0

First Kensington Trade Paperback Printing: July 2025

10 9 8 7 6 5 4 3 2 1

Printed in the United States of America

The authorized representative in the EU for product safety and compliance is eucomply OU, Parnu mnt 139b-14, Apt 123
Tallinn, Berlin 11317, hello@eucompliancepartner.com

Contents

One Lonesome Cowboy

LINDA LAEL MILLER

For John Scognamiglio,
with love and appreciation

Prologue

Chicago, Illinois

Susannah Holiday pressed her smartphone to her ear and her gray and black tabby cat, Nico, to her side as she listened to the caller's voice. Distinctly female, the sound seemed to fade in and out, as though it were crackling its way from a distant galaxy, bouncing from one planet to another, rather than some satellite orbiting the Earth.

"Your sister, Rebecca Bennet—psychiatric ward—child in temporary care of a friend—"

Hot tears scalded Susannah's eyes, and she blinked them back. Sucked in a steadying breath, and loosened her grip on Nico.

He leapt, with a low and indignant meow, to the kitchen floor and, tail bristling, sashayed his way out of the room.

Susannah leaned against the counter and shoved a hand through her dark shoulder-length hair. The pain reminded her that she was wearing a ponytail that morning.

"Yes," she managed, after a small inner struggle. "Yes, I'm

Becky's—Rebecca's—sister, actually. Her only living relative, besides little Ellie."

Ellie. Susannah's heart ached for the child. She'd been abandoned by her no-account father several years before, and Becky, though she loved her daughter fiercely, was fragile emotionally.

Three years older than Susannah, Becky had struggled with mental health since middle school. She'd suffered some trauma back then, one she refused to discuss, even with her therapists, evidently.

A stab of guilt knifed through Susannah.

I should have done more.

But what?

Becky hadn't been willing to confide in her; no matter how much she'd pleaded, cajoled, and finally nagged, that one mysterious area of Becky's life had remained inaccessible.

She'd helped Becky and Ellie in other ways, especially financially, for a long time, pitching in for rent or groceries now and then, and even paid for Becky's intermittent counseling sessions, but that obviously hadn't been enough.

Susannah supposed she should have joined her sister and her niece in the small town of Copper Ridge, Arizona, long ago, but she'd loved living in the busy buzz of Chicago; she had friends here, a business creating websites, and a thriving sidehustle, flipping houses.

"We've placed Ellie with a local couple, Jack and Harper O'Ballivan, for the time being," the female voice droned on, professional, smooth, without inflection. "Mrs. O'Ballivan works as a counselor in the school Ellie attends, so they're acquainted. The O'Ballivans are reputable people and they are willing to serve as foster parents to her if needed. That said, we usually prefer to place a child with a responsible family member, if at all possible, which is why we are contacting you."

"Of course." Susannah was shivering, even though that day

in early June was sunny and warm, verging on hot. "I'll be there as soon as I can make arrangements." She stiffened her spine, turned to grab a glass from the cupboard, filled it from the tap. Drank thirstily. "Could you tell me again how Becky is doing? Which hospital she's in? I'm afraid I missed some of what you said at first. I was in shock, I think."

"Certainly, Ms. Holiday." The woman waited politely, having guessed, it seemed, that Susannah was scrabbling in a drawer for a notepad and pen.

"I'm ready," Susannah said, when she was.

As the social worker spoke, Susannah scribbled down the details.

The conversation ended, and Susannah's first call was to her preferred airline.

She booked a flight for midafternoon.

Her second was to a company that specialized in transporting vehicles and other belongings from one place to another. She would need her practical SUV when she reached Arizona, though she planned to use a rental car until it arrived, and she couldn't leave her desktop behind, either.

Practically her entire life was on that computer.

In the interim, she could use her laptop to keep up with her current design projects and the duplex she was renovating in one of the city's leafy suburbs.

The last call, before she hauled out her suitcases and Nico's much-despised cat-carrier, was to Harper O'Ballivan, the woman looking after Ellie. She introduced herself and asked if this was a good time to speak to her niece.

There was a warm smile in Harper's voice. "Absolutely," she replied. "She's right here. School's out, as of yesterday, and Ellie and I have been baking cookies this morning. We'll be taking some to her mom, after lunch."

Susannah's throat knotted with emotion. "Thank you," she said, with an effort.

"No problem," Harper answered.

And then Ellie was on the line. "Auntie Susannah?" she asked tentatively.

Ellie was twelve, as of her last birthday, but she sounded much younger.

"None other," Susannah confirmed, forcing a positive note. "I'm on my way, sweetheart. I know this is a scary situation, but we'll handle this together—you, me and your mom. Everything will be all right, I promise."

While she awaited her niece's response, Susannah offered a silent but fervent prayer that she'd be able to keep her word.

There was sweet relief in Ellie's sigh. "Okay," she said.

"You're safe there, where you are? With the O'Ballivans? You can use our secret word if you're not. Do you remember it?"

"Yes," Ellie answered, sounding stronger. "But we don't need it. Mr. and Mrs. O'Ballivan are really nice. They're doing lots of stuff to help Mom, and me, too. And Gideon is teaching me to ride ponies. He's their son."

Susannah's weighted heart lifted a little. "Good. I'll see you soon, honey."

"Are you bringing Nico?" The question was cautiously hopeful. Nico and Ellie had established a friendly relationship during her and Becky's last visit to Chicago, six months before.

"Yes," she answered, without hesitation. Nico could be a first-class furry butthead, but Susannah loved him without reservation. She'd rescued him, as a mewling, half-starved kitten, when she'd seen him tossed from a car parked along a roadside and then left behind.

A mental checklist was forming in her mind.

Of course she'd have to pack some clothes, cosmetics and toiletry items, devices and chargers, etc.

And stop off at the vet's office for a last-minute health check and a sedative for Nico, so—hopefully—the feisty feline wouldn't yowl pitifully throughout the flight to Flagstaff and drive the passengers and crew around the bend.

For the moment, though, Nico's potential disruptive behavior was the least of Susannah's worries.

She needed to get to her sister and her niece.

Fast.

Chapter 1

Ian McKenzie stood on the deck of his modest ranch house, watching as the pickup truck turned off the main road, loaded horse trailer bumping along behind it, and labored up the dirt driveway.

Six horses this time.

Ian strode toward the corral and, reaching it, swung open the gate.

Clouds of dust billowed in the soft heat of that June morning while Knute Carlson, an animal lover and good friend to Ian, tooted the horn in greeting and then maneuvered the truck and trailer, backing up to the corral entrance.

Meanwhile, Ian's aging three-legged dog, Dub, confined to the kitchen, barked frantically from behind the sliding glass door on the deck, desperate to get out of the house and join in whatever ruckus might arise.

Or to cause one.

Ignoring the dog, Ian met Knute when he climbed out of that rattle-trap old truck and thrust out a hand in greeting.

"Mornin', Ian," Knute responded, extending his own hand.

"Me and Erma sure do appreciate you taking on these poor critters. Our barn is full-up and the pasture's getting crowded, too, now that we're running a few cattle on the place."

"Glad to help," Ian replied, his voice a little gruff. He knew every horse in that trailer had suffered, and the thought always choked him up.

Knute gave him a knowing look. He, too, felt deep sympathy for mistreated or injured animals; that was why he did his level best to look after them.

Knute and his wife, Erma, were big-hearted folks, both retired from their long-term factory jobs, and instead of kicking back and enjoying their free time, they'd immediately decided to devote whatever might remain of their lives to rescuing horses.

Ian's respect for them ran deep, and it was solid as bedrock.

Knute was starting to slow down physically, though, but Ian knew it was no use asking him to step aside and let him, Ian, unload the horses this time around. The old man was too proud to allow that.

Knute grinned, adjusted his battered baseball cap, and rounded the trailer to lower the steel ramp, open the door and step inside.

The horses were agitated, and there was a lot of stomping and neighing going on. If they were stirred up enough to start kicking, Knute could be trampled, cut to pieces by flying hooves, or both.

Ian silently reminded himself that his friend had a lot of experience wrangling horses. Besides, he himself was a paramedic, and his equipment was nearby, stashed in the back of his own truck—but that didn't do much to ease his worries about Knute's safety.

Back in the house, Dub was still barking his brains out.

Ian shook his head and waited.

Sure enough, Knute put halters on each of the horses, one

by one, and led them down the ramp from the trailer. Then Ian led them into the corral, where the water trough was full and the feeders bristled with fresh, fragrant hay, removed their halters, and examined them for injuries or signs of disease.

All six of them were mares, which simplified things a little. Geldings were all right, but stallions, especially wild ones, were another matter. In the years he'd been rescuing, training and re-homing these animals, he'd dealt with every known variation—kickers, biters, belly-to-the-sky buckers.

And he'd loved every one of them. Ached inside when new and carefully vetted owners arrived to lead them back into horse trailers and haul them away to a new home.

"You off work the whole day?" Knute asked, once the trailer was empty, dragging an arm across his sweating forehead and readjusting his ball cap again.

"Four days on, three days off," Ian explained. He'd outlined his work schedule to Knute more than once, but he could see no reason to point that out. If his friend was getting a little forgetful as he aged, well, that was normal, wasn't it?

"Erma's hoping you can come to our place for Sunday dinner," Knute ventured. "I reckon she's looking to introduce you to another of her younger friends from church."

Ian grinned, though he was careful not to let Knute see. He was happy with his life as it was, for the time being, and he didn't see any point in beating the figurative brush for another spouse.

He and Catherine, his former wife, were still friends, though they didn't see each other often. She'd remarried six months ago, but fortunately, she still sent Ian's nine-year-old twin stepdaughters, Mabel and Vivian, to spend six weeks of the summer with him, on his small ranch just outside of Copper Ridge.

He loved those children as his own, since they'd been toddlers when he and Catherine met and married. Since their father had died in a car accident two months before they were born, Ian had been the only father they'd ever known.

And they were due to arrive Sunday morning.

He planned to welcome them with a houseful of banners and balloons and maybe a few presents, though every visit was preceded by an email or phone call from Catherine, warning him not to spoil the twins.

"I wish I could join you," Ian said, and that was true. Erma's cooking was stellar, and the regular gatherings at her and Knute's well-maintained double-wide on their small farm were lively and a lot of fun, Erma's constant matchmaking aside. "But I'll be headed for the Flagstaff airport to pick up the kids that morning."

Knute grinned. "Well, that's as good a reason as any to miss out on Erma's lasagna pizza," he told Ian, with a note of jovial letdown in his voice. "But you know what my dear wife would say if she was here: Bring 'em. There's always room at our table."

Regretfully, Ian shook his head. He was watching the horses out of the corner of one eye: five were crowded around the feeders, but the sixth stood, head drooping, in a far corner of the corral.

That one would need extra care. Immediately.

Otherwise, the tattered little mare might become a scape-goat.

"Some other time, Knute," he said. "The kids will need to settle in after the flight from Miami, and I haven't seen them since Christmas, so we'll have some catching up to do."

This last part was something of a stretch, since Ian was on FaceTime with his daughters twice a week, so he saw them pretty regularly. Problem was, communicating online wasn't the same as being with them in person.

Knute let the subject go at that, shook Ian's hand again, then slid the ramp back in place under the trailer, closed and latched the door and ambled around to the driver's side door of his truck.

With a nod of farewell, the older man climbed into the seat with admirable agility, for a man more than twice Ian's age—started the rumbling engine, and drove off down the driveway.

Before turning back onto the road, he honked again.

Ian chuckled to himself and waved.

Then he climbed over the corral fence and approached the shivering little mare, every movement slow and—he hoped—reassuring to the frightened animal.

"Hey, Ragamuffin," he greeted her gently, extending a hand for her to sniff with her velvety nose.

The mare shuffled backwards, only to bump into the fence behind her.

"Easy," Ian whispered. "You're safe now. Nobody's going to hurt you."

She nickered, tossed her head in a slight motion that nevertheless indicated that there was still spirit, somewhere inside her.

He stood with her for a long time, stroking her bony sides when she'd allow it, murmuring tender gibberish.

After fifteen minutes or so, he put a halter on her and she allowed him to lead her into the barn.

It was shadowy and cool inside, smelling pleasantly of grain and straw and saddle soap, despite the inevitable undercurrent of manure.

His own horses—the "keepers," he called them—were out grazing in a nearby pasture, which was probably a plus, given how nervous the little mare was, even after the time he'd spent comforting her.

Chipwick and Apple Pie, the black and white spotted ponies the twins rode when they visited, probably wouldn't have kicked up a fuss at the newcomer's arrival, though they'd have a thing or two to say about the other five coming in later on to fill the empty stalls.

Ian's powerful palomino gelding, Sultan, knew he was the head honcho, and he paid little or no attention to the barn-mates who came and went. Mostly.

He'd tangled with a young stallion a year ago, another visitor, Sultan had, but, though he'd come out the winner, he had a few scars to remember the incident by. Other than that, and the usual challenges of training any horse, let alone the mistrustful sort, there hadn't been a lot of trouble.

Reaching the enclosure he'd chosen for the ragamuffin, Ian brought his thoughts back to the matter at hand, opened the stall door, and carefully led the hesitant mare inside.

He removed the halter, set it aside, made sure the automatic waterer was up and running, and loaded the feeder with hay and a couple of scoops of grain. Then, when the mare, after much sniffing, finally began to eat, he gently brushed her down.

As he groomed her, he was careful to avoid several scabbed-over cuts on her legs and haunches, and when he'd finished with that, he washed the marks with as much tenderness as he would have shown an injured human being.

Then he applied salve.

He checked each of her hooves for wounds, removed a few small stones and other minor detritus.

He'd need to call the farrier and have her hooves trimmed, along with those of the five other mares, but that could wait a day or two.

When he'd finished tending to the skinny female, he went back to the house and released Dub from the confines of the kitchen, where he'd been not-so-patiently waiting ever since Knute's arrival over an hour before.

Lean and gray, with floppy ears and plenty of muscle, Dub was a faithful companion, and Ian felt a twinge of chagrin for having left him inside, but Dub wasn't one to hold grudges.

He trotted alongside Ian as he headed back toward the corral, moving as nimbly as if he hadn't been short a leg.

"These critters are new here, and they're probably a little scared, so be nice," Ian told the dog, as they walked. Because he was alone a lot, and because he worked with animals all the time, Ian was beyond any concern about his habit of chatting with—or at—the furry contingent.

He'd grown up around dogs, cats, horses, pigs and cattle; in fact, the small but fertile ranch he lived on had belonged to his late grandparents, and he'd spent summers, weekends and holidays right here.

After college, he'd trained as a paramedic, living down south in Phoenix, and it was there that he'd met and eventually married Catherine.

As he attended to each of the other mares, leading them to their stalls and brushing them down, he thought about his ex-wife, who was a prosecuting attorney in Florida, where she'd moved after their awkward but amicable divorce.

They'd been married for five years, still living and working in Phoenix, where they'd both landed well-paying jobs.

Catherine was a good-looking woman, a natural blonde, smart and fit and very, very ambitious. Looking back, Ian wasn't sure if he'd truly loved her, or if he'd actually loved the *idea* of her. After all, she was attractive, and she came with two adorable daughters, a ready-made family.

And that was what Ian had wanted most in life—a loving wife, kids, a home, a dog or two. A career that mattered.

When had the relationship begun to fall apart?

He wasn't sure, since it had happened gradually.

His grandfather had died, and six months later, his grandmother followed.

Ian's parents, long-divorced and very involved in their separate, fast-track lives, hadn't bothered to attend either funeral, and the contents of the old folks' wills probably seemed paltry to them. Too paltry to even ask about.

As it turned out, Ian had inherited everything—the ranch,

significant mineral rights, and the combined life savings of two hardworking people.

He'd visited the ranch several times after they were gone, well aware that Catherine expected him to sell the place and move on.

It wasn't that they'd needed the money; between his job as a paramedic and sometime firefighter and Catherine's as a promising young lawyer, they'd had enough. But it eventually became apparent that their personal goals had shifted.

Even after months of soul-searching, Ian wasn't able to give up the ranch; he had roots there, and they went deep. He wanted to live on that familiar land with Catherine and the kids, build on to the house, rebuild the weathered barn. And maybe add to their family, too.

As small as the nearby town of Copper Ridge was, there were opportunities for Catherine, as well as Ian himself. She could have set up a private practice, made new friends, traveled when time allowed.

Country life would have been good for the kids, too. They could grow up riding horses, going fishing, camping out. The less they stared at the screens on their fancy phones, the better.

From the first, though, Catherine wasn't having it.

She'd never lived in the country, and she didn't intend to start. She liked cities, with all their hustle-bustle and excitement and opportunity. And she'd changed her mind about having more children somewhere along the way, without telling Ian — deciding that the twins didn't need siblings. They'd been preemies, born after a very rough pregnancy, and she hadn't wanted to take the risk — or let her career be stuck in neutral for months, if not years.

He understood but the arguments didn't stop.

They'd yelled when the kids weren't around and whispered furiously when they were.

Then Catherine was offered a job with a big-time law firm in a suburb of Miami, thanks to her wide network of friends from college and law school, and that was it.

With tears of both sorrow and relief, Ian and Catherine had agreed to separate legally, and follow their divergent dreams. Catherine would take the children and move to Miami. Ian would live on his ranch and work as a paramedic.

After a year, per their mutual agreement, they would meet on neutral ground—in New Orleans, as it turned out—and decide whether they would reconcile or file for divorce. Since neither of them wanted to live anywhere but where they were, or give up their lifestyles, they decided to end the marriage.

As divorces go, theirs was an easy one, compared to the knock-down-drag-outs Catherine had described during her early career.

The hardest part for Ian was no longer seeing his girls.

There had never been any question of custody; the twins would stay with their biological mother, though Ian could see them whenever he wanted to, and the girls, in turn, would spend time with their stepfather every summer, with the occasional shorter visit allowed, when possible and convenient for both parents.

It was all so freaking *reasonable.*

Except it wasn't. It was hell, at least for Ian.

But, then, when did life ever turn out the way a person expected it to?

Mabel and Vivian, seven years old at the time of the split, had been devastated.

They'd cried in protest, each of them hanging onto one of Ian's legs as he'd left the house in Phoenix for the last time.

He'd cried, too, once he was alone in his truck. Hell, he'd *sobbed,* and pounded the steering wheel with one fist. Fought the urge to go back inside, tell Catherine he'd changed his mind, that he'd sell the ranch and forget all about it, and move to Florida with her and the girls after all.

Trouble was, he couldn't do that.

As much as he loved Catherine and his stepdaughters, he knew giving in would be a mistake. He didn't *belong* in Miami, and Catherine didn't belong on a small ranch outside a small town.

No matter who won the tug of war, they wouldn't have been able to sustain the love they felt for each other.

It was Dub who brought Ian back from his mental sojourn, with a little whine and a nudge.

All the horses were settled in for the night, including the pair of ponies and Sultan, his gelding.

The western sky flared with flashes of orange and apricot, pink and purple.

Ian shoved a hand through his dark brown hair and drank in the beauty of that scene.

It was time to shower, change clothes and think about supper.

Chapter 2

A young orderly with a buzz cut and multiple tattoos on his forearms led Susannah through passage after passage, corridor after corridor of Northern Arizona Community Hospital until, finally, they stood before a thick metal door marked "Staff Only."

Expecting to be left in the hallway, Susannah sucked in and released several deep breaths, trying to steady herself.

She *had* to see her sister, but she felt unprepared. Out of her depth.

Becky had been through some rocky times emotionally, but she'd never been institutionalized.

Susannah automatically looked away while the orderly punched in a series of numbers on a panel next to the door.

A loud *clunk* sounded, and the lock was disengaged.

"Here we go," said the orderly, turning to Susannah. "Your sister"—he paused, pulled a small tablet out of a pocket of his scrubs, consulted it—"Rebecca Bennet? Is that correct?"

"Yes," Susannah replied, anxious and eager, both at the same time. "She goes by Becky."

The orderly ignored that tidbit of information. "This way. We're heading for the patients' lounge."

Instead of following, Susannah managed to come alongside her escort, and out of the corner of her eye, she glimpsed his name tag.

Tanner Beaumont.

Doors lined the next corridor they passed through.

The silence was thick and strangely muffled.

She closed her eyes briefly and sent a silent prayer heavenward.

Keep Becky safe. Please.

"Mr. Beaumont?" she ventured, after another deep breath.

"Tanner," the young man corrected pleasantly, waiting.

Susannah squared her shoulders and lifted her chin. "Is my sister safe here?"

Tanner smiled. "Absolutely," he said.

Susannah wished she could be so confident. But maybe she would be, after she'd seen her sister with her own eyes, knew how she was being looked after.

The large, arched doorway leading into the lounge was graced on either side by healthy ficus trees in enormous pots, and the sounds coming from beyond the entrance were blessedly ordinary—classical music, played softly, quiet conversations, the occasional burst of laughter.

Entering the large space, Susannah saw patients everywhere.

Some were sipping tea or coffee at one of the long tables.

Some were snoozing peacefully in armchairs.

She swept the room, spotted Becky right away.

Her sister sat in a wheelchair beside a tall window, staring blankly into space, her blonde hair and fragile frame rimmed in sunlight. The sight of her made Susannah think of a lost angel.

Her heart pinched hard and then lodged itself in her throat. The backs of her eyes stung with tears she was determined not to shed until she was alone in her hotel room in Copper Ridge, where she'd dropped off her suitcases and settled Nico in for a rest. Hopefully, he would behave himself in the interim.

No matter what, she couldn't risk upsetting Becky by giving in to her own turbulent emotions, not when her sister was so vulnerable.

After a brief nod of thanks to Tanner, Susannah crossed the room, zigzagging her way between patients, chairs, smaller tables and wheelchairs, some inhabited, some empty.

Reaching Becky, she gently laid a hand on her sister's bony shoulder. She was wearing a plain terry-cloth bathrobe over a green cotton hospital gown, and her usually lustrous hair was dull, pulled back into a ponytail at her nape.

"Becky," Susannah whispered, barely able to wedge the words past the lump lingering in her throat. "It's me, Susannah. I'm here, and I'll stick around as long as you and Ellie need me."

Becky's pale blue eyes remained expressionless, fixed on something no one else could see.

Sternly renewing her resolution not to break down and sob, Susannah grabbed a nearby folding chair and set it directly in front of her shattered sister.

She sat down, and their knees were almost touching, but if Becky knew Susannah was there, she gave no indication of it.

In her mind, Susannah reviewed the little information she'd been able to gather, when she'd spoken to Becky's attending physician over the phone.

She'd outlined Becky's medical history as best she could, and Dr. Mowgat, a gentle and refined-sounding woman of obvious intelligence, had listened carefully.

After explaining that Becky had had problems with her mental health since her early teens, though none of them had required hospitalization—only counseling and medication— she'd asked Dr. Mowgat for her impressions.

The doctor had replied that "Ms. Bennet" had suffered a

"nervous collapse" while at home. Her young daughter had become concerned by her condition and dialed 911.

Paramedics had hurried to the house, soon followed by several local police officers, and found Becky in an unresponsive state. They'd examined her and then brought her to the nearest hospital, Northern Arizona Community, which was halfway between Flagstaff and Copper Ridge.

After more examination and numerous medical tests, Becky had been admitted.

Now, sitting across from her sister, Susannah ached with sorrow. She and Becky were actually half sisters, with the same mother and different fathers, but they'd always been close.

Not so close, Susannah reminded herself, that Becky had ever confided in her.

Whatever *had* happened, it had traumatized her terribly, that long ago summer of her thirteenth year. Susannah had been ten at the time.

Since then, Becky had remained unstable emotionally, and she'd endured cycles of depression so severe that she couldn't get out of bed.

Eventually, she'd become seriously involved with a rowdy deadbeat named Roy Pendleton, and sweet little Ellie had been the product of that chaotic entanglement. As far as Susannah knew, the two had never married, and Becky still went by her maiden name, Bennet.

Much of Becky's life was a mystery. She clearly loved her daughter, but she had few friends and, much of the time, she hadn't been able to hold down a job for more than a month or two. She was a hard worker, but she tended to lapse into periods of all-consuming inertia.

They sat in silence for a long time.

Watching Becky, Susannah had to steel herself over and over again, to fight back torrents of tears. She felt so damnably *helpless*, and, love her sister though she did, as desperate as she was to help her, a part of Susannah wanted to grab the woman by her thin shoulders and shake her, hard, yelling, *What happened? Damn it, Becky, tell me what happened!*

Of course that wasn't an option.

So, finally, she took Becky's limp, cool hands into her own, leaned in and said, very softly, "Let someone, *anyone*, help you. If you won't recover for yourself, do it for Ellie."

Becky's light eyelashes fluttered then, and her chin wobbled.

Susannah held her breath, waiting.

"Ellie," Becky said, in what amounted to a whisper. *"Ellie."*

Before Susannah could respond, Tanner was back, standing beside Susannah's chair, resting a hand briefly on her shoulder.

"Time's up," he said gently. "Ms. Bennet needs to rest."

Susannah understood the protocol, knew it was all in the best interest of the patients. So, though she wasn't ready to leave Becky, she nodded and rose to her feet.

Before walking away, she leaned down and kissed her sister on the top of her head. "Don't worry about Ellie," she told her quietly. "I've got this."

Fifteen minutes later, she was in her rental car again, pointed in the direction of Copper Ridge, and though she'd looked forward to finally letting her guard down and sobbing until her eyes were raw, crying and driving didn't mix.

So she took more deep breaths as she drove, and thought about the next step: picking Ellie up at the O'Ballivans' place and taking her—where? To the small house she and Becky had been living in for the past six years? To her own hotel room in Copper Ridge?

She couldn't decide.

So she simply kept driving.

The roads there in Arizona's high country were winding and, unlike the southern parts of the state, thickly lined with scrub-brush and evergreen trees. Even more reason to concentrate.

She had just rounded a long, wide turn when it happened.

A saddled horse ran across the road, full-speed, reins dangling.

Susannah braked and looked around quickly. *Where was the rider?*

Carefully, her heart pounding, she pulled to the side of the road, unfastened her seat belt and climbed out to stand on the pavement.

The horse was slowing down, which was probably good, but there was still no sign of the rider. Surely there *was* a rider, since the animal was equipped with a saddle and bridle.

"Hello?" Susannah cried, cupping her hands around her mouth. "Is anyone there?"

She paused to listen then and, sure enough, a voice sounded from somewhere in the brush, on the left side of the road.

"I'm—here—"

Susannah plunged into the thicket of grass lining the ditch, slipping on the rocks and flailing for balance. "I'm coming," she called out, moving into the woods.

She found the boy in a small clearing, sprawled on the ground. He was a kid, no older than fourteen or fifteen, with blond hair, and hazel eyes now squinched in pain.

Dropping to her knees beside him, Susannah fumbled in her jeans pocket for her phone, dialed 911.

A little breathless from all the dashing around, she did her best to convey the location and describe the boy's condition.

First question from the dispatcher: "Is he breathing?"

"Yes," Susannah replied, all but gasping the word. Then, addressing the boy, who was stirring slightly on the rocky ground, "Don't move!"

"I have to catch my horse," the kid protested.

He was bleeding from the back of his head, and one of his legs lay at an angle that made Susannah cringe inwardly. She shushed him and turned her attention back to the dispatcher. "I think he was thrown from a horse—yes—I'm sure he's hurt."

For the boy's sake, she didn't describe his condition.

"Paramedics on the way," the dispatcher said, after Susannah had done her best to describe the location. "What kind of vehicle are you driving?"

"It's a white compact, a rental with Arizona plates—parked on the side of the road." The words tumbled out of Susannah's mouth; the boy was moaning now, writhing in pain. "Tell them to hurry! Please!"

"Try to stay calm, ma'am," the dispatcher urged easily. He—or she—Susannah couldn't quite tell which—was clearly used to calls like this one. And it was part of their job to keep it together in any kind of crisis.

"Want me to stay on the line with you?"

Susannah shook her head before realizing she had to respond verbally, since she and the dispatcher weren't on Face-Time. "I think we'll be all right here until the ambulance arrives. If there's a problem in the meantime, I'll call you back."

"Excellent," the dispatcher replied, and the call ended.

Susannah laid her phone on the ground and spoke as evenly and quietly as she could. "What's your name?" she asked. "I'll call your folks and let them know you've been hurt."

"Tim," the boy answered, between groans. "Tim Boyd. My—mom and—dad—are working—"

"You must know their numbers."

Tim tried to shake his head and stopped, with a wince. "I just press—these buttons—"

"Where's your phone?" Susannah asked, sounding much more with-it than she felt. Inside, she was churning with anxiety.

Tim tried to laugh but that, like the attempt to shake his head, was a bust. "Under me," he said, after a struggle.

She didn't dare move him, even to retrieve his phone. The paramedics, or the hospital admissions people, would have to notify the parents.

Minutes passed.

Susannah made a quick scramble up to the road, to get a box of tissues from the car. Damn! If she'd been driving her own SUV, there would have been an emergency blanket and a first-aid kit. Plus, her suitcases were back at the hotel, so she couldn't grab a T-shirt or a beach towel to help stanch the bleeding.

There was one good thing, anyway: The horse had returned.

It stood, reins dragging, head down, maybe twenty yards from the rental car.

Susannah felt a pang of sympathy for the animal. Was it hurt?

She didn't have time to find out, since Tim was still lying where he'd fallen.

She went back to the boy, found the tissues insufficient against the bleeding, and was considering hauling her T-shirt off over her head and using it as a compress when she heard the piercing, not-too-distant sound of a siren.

Susannah sat back on the heels of her sneakers, closed her eyes and thanked God.

Tim was pale, and his eyes were unfocused, so he was probably about to lose consciousness.

"Stay with me, Tim," she pleaded.

"My—horse—" he groaned.

"Your horse came back." A pause. "He looks okay."

Another siren intertwined itself with the first.

Tears of sheer relief stung Susannah's eyes. "Hear that? That's the ambulance. Help will be here any minute now."

Tim closed his eyes and seemed to sink into himself, and Susannah gripped his wrist, feeling for a pulse. He was still alive, but his heartbeat was weak.

She knew that from the first aid classes she'd taken back in college.

Bending low to whisper in the boy's ear, Susannah nearly choked on the metallic scent of the blood he was shedding at a frightening rate. When applying pressure didn't work, she was forced to change course.

"I'll be right back," she promised.

Then she made another rushed and arduous journey up to the road.

Spotting the ambulance in the near distance, she waved both arms, just in case the medics didn't see her.

Which was silly, of course, but she was barely able to control her panic.

Tim's horse, meanwhile, spooked by the shrill noise of the sirens, and probably the flashing lights as well, was prancing and snorting and tossing his head.

Knowing less than nothing about horses, Susannah nevertheless approached the terrified animal and caught hold of its bridle strap with one hand.

"Hush!" she commanded the frantic creature.

Miraculously, the horse began to settle down a little.

Susannah held on. Watched and waited as first the ambulance lurched to a stop nearby, then the police car.

A man and a woman climbed down from their seats in the cab of the emergency vehicle and hurried around to open the doors at the back of the ambulance.

They were both in uniform, carrying the stretcher they'd yanked out of the rig. Blessedly, they'd turned off the sirens by then, though the red and blue lights were still splashing around and around, dizzyingly bright.

"Where's the kid?" asked the police officer, a man in his mid-fifties, with graying hair and sharp eyes. His name tag read, "Sgt. Jim Wallis. Copper Ridge Police Department."

Susannah pointed toward the trees, still holding on the horse's bridle, lest the animal run away again. Her arm and shoulder ached from the effort.

The paramedics were already hustling down into the brush, toward Tim.

Calmly, the policeman took the horse's reins from Susannah and tied them loosely to the door handle on the driver's side of his cruiser. "I know the people who own this fella. I'll give them a call, and they'll be here with a trailer in no time."

"I guess that's the benefit of living in a small community like Copper Ridge," Susannah said, and then felt stupid. "I mean, everybody knows everybody, right?"

The officer smiled patiently, and that eased Susannah's tension a bit.

"Boy's name is Tim Boyd?" he asked.

"Yes. I was going to call his parents, but he said he didn't remember their numbers and his phone was under him and I didn't want to move him so—"

"It's all right, Ms.—"

"Holiday. Susannah Holiday. I'm Becky Bennet's sister."

TMI? Susannah didn't know, and didn't care.

Jim Wallis gave a brisk nod. "I was real sorry to hear about Becky's troubles." He sounded sincere, and took a small notebook from the shirt pocket of his uniform, along with a pen. "Now, can you tell me exactly what happened here, Ms. Holiday?"

Trembling now, as the worst of the shock began to subside, Susannah related the story.

Just as she was finishing, a pickup pulling a horse trailer rounded a bend and drew up behind Susannah's rental.

A hefty older man wearing overalls and a billed cap stepped down from the driver's seat and approached.

"Hello, Knute," Officer Wallis said cordially. "Your horse isn't hurt, far as I can tell."

Knute nodded a hello at Susannah and approached the fitful horse.

Skillfully, he bent and ran work-callused hands over the animal's limbs, and when he straightened, he was smiling.

Susannah let out a long breath, relieved.

"Thanks for the call, Jim," the old man said, untying the animal and leading it toward the truck and trailer. "I placed this rascal with the Boyds a month or so ago," he continued, speaking over one shoulder. "For their son Tim, you know. I reckon that boy's gone and gotten hurt?"

The policeman nodded. "Got himself thrown," he said. "Ian and Marva are down there now, scraping him up off the ground."

Susannah winced inwardly at the picture this statement brought to mind.

Oddly, though, her attention snagged on a name.

Ian. The paramedic.

Susannah had gotten a good look at him, but for the briefest moment, as he passed her with one end of the stretcher under his arm, their eyes had met.

His were a dark, denim blue, full of gentle intelligence and confidence in his ability to handle whatever had to be handled.

Now, she realized she liked the man, though technically they hadn't met.

How could that have happened?

The man called Knute was loading Tim Boyd's horse into the trailer. Presently, he closed the trailer's doors and got back into his pickup truck.

With a toot of his horn, he drove away.

After another fifteen minutes, the paramedics reappeared, carrying the stretcher, with the young boy loosely but expertly strapped to it.

Tim's head was bandaged; he'd been hooked up to an IV, and his broken leg was in a temporary splint.

He looked as though he was unconscious; he'd turned a shade of bluish gray, and Susannah was horrified all over again.

"Is he dead?" she croaked, before pressing one hand to her mouth. Her lunch, purchased at a drive-through just outside Flagstaff, immediately after she'd left the airport, was suddenly roiling in her stomach, threatening to come back up, then and there.

Officer Wallis was on his phone, most likely explaining the situation to one of Tim's parents.

The female paramedic, Marva, was a sturdy, muscular type, with a kind face. She shook her head sympathetically, but said nothing.

There were several ways to interpret the gesture, and Susannah turned her anxious gaze to the man, Ian.

He smiled at her, and for a moment, it was as if half a dozen different dimensions had collided, woven themselves into strands and finally become one.

Something intangible passed between them, something Susannah couldn't begin to define *or* describe, and she wavered on her feet, dizzy. So dizzy that she thought she might actually faint.

"He's going to be all right," Ian said, watching her closely. "We're taking him to Community, just up the road, and he'll probably be there a while. If you want, you can call in later, so someone can fill you in."

Susannah was still trying to collect herself.

It had all been too much—flying down from Chicago in what amounted to a rush, driving to Copper Ridge with a squalling cat scratching angrily at the opening to his carrier in the back seat, checking into the hotel, then, after dropping off both her bags and a much calmer Nico, doubling back almost halfway to Flagstaff to see Becky, and finding her in a nearly comatose condition. All that, and Tim's accident, too.

Ian and his coworker were busy loading patient and stretcher into the back of the ambulance. After that, Ian climbed into the back with Tim, while Marva made her way to the driver's seat.

Officer Wallis was on his radio, calling in the details of the accident.

Still feeling slightly out of sync with herself, Susannah walked back to her car.

Officer Wallis waved a farewell.

As the ambulance went into a wide U-turn, the siren came back on.

Susannah sat behind the wheel of the rental, sipping lukewarm water from a bottle she'd pulled from her purse, trying to get it together enough to drive safely back to Copper Ridge and all the problems waiting to be solved.

Chapter 3

The twins, escorted through airport security by a cheerful flight attendant, scanned the waiting crowd with wide eyes, their grins expectant and full of a delight that made Ian's heart skip several beats.

He extended his arms, and Mabel and Vivian raced toward him, their blonde curls bobbing around their bright faces and their matching pink backpacks bouncing with every step.

"Daddy!" they chorused as he bent to gather them close.

He kissed the tops of their heads and blinked back the tears brimming in his eyes while they clung to him, their arms circling his waist.

The flight attendant, an attractive middle-aged woman with bright red hair, smiled as she took in the happy reunion.

"It's obvious that you're Ian McKenzie," she said, after consulting the screen of her smartphone, "but I still need to see your identification. Company policy."

Ian nodded. Smiled.

It took some maneuvering to get his wallet out of his back pocket, with both his daughters still holding on to him as though he were a life raft in the middle of a turbulent sea, but he managed and showed the flight attendant his ID.

Using her phone again, the woman scanned the card quickly, then handed it back. "Thank you, Mr. McKenzie."

"Thank you," he replied, "for keeping my daughters safe."

With that, they parted.

After untangling the girls from his middle, Ian headed for the baggage claim area, holding their hands. "How was the flight?" he asked, feeling so happy that he wasn't sure the soles of his boots were touching the floor.

"It was looooong," Mabel replied, gazing up at Ian as she spoke and rolling her bright green eyes.

"Don't forget to text Mom that we're here," Vivian piped up.

Ian stopped, took his phone from the clip on his belt, and obeyed.

Catherine was an exceptional mother, and she would be waiting for confirmation.

She replied almost immediately with a heart emoji and **Don't spoil them, Ian. I'm serious!**

Ian sent a thumbs-up and put his phone away.

The twins chattered incessantly as the three of them waited for their suitcases, each expensive-looking bag featuring a different brightly colored Disney princess. And Catherine was worried that *he* would spoil these kids?

Once they reached the parking area, and the suitcases had been stowed in the bed of Ian's truck, the girls scrambled into the back seat and immediately fastened their seat belts.

"You didn't bring Dub?" Mabel asked, clearly disappointed.

Behind the wheel by then, Ian shook his head. "You know dogs shouldn't be left alone in a vehicle for any length of time. Kids, either. Especially not in Arizona."

"Yeah," Vivian said, making a face at her sister, who was her mirror image. "Every year kids and animals *die* because they got left in a hot car. *Keep up*, Mabel."

"That'll do, girls," Ian said mildly, starting the truck, shifting into gear and joining the line of cars and other pickups heading for the nearest exit. Argument averted. "Are you hungry?"

"No," said Mabel.

"We ate on the plane," clarified Vivian.

"Mom's new husband is a pilot, so we got to sit in first class," Mabel added.

Ian smiled to himself. Concentrated on navigating the traffic as they left the airport for the main highway.

Catherine's new husband.

At one time, that phrase would have stung; now, all he could think about was how glad he was to be with his daughters again, live and in person. FaceTime was a lifesaver, but it couldn't compete with *real* time.

As for Catherine, well, he hoped she would be genuinely happy, now that she'd evidently found the right someone.

Ian gave a barely audible sigh. He'd been pretty lonesome, at times, and though he'd dated a few women since the divorce, he hadn't really connected with any of them.

What would it be like to have a wife again? A true partner and soulmate?

For no reason he could put his finger on, the image of the woman he'd encountered the day before, at the scene of the horse-and-rider accident, bloomed in his mind, vivid and clear. He hadn't been scheduled for duty, but Dennis Meyer, who usually teamed up with Marva Hills, had called in sick, so Ian had covered for him.

Her name, Jim Wallis had told him later—after young Tim Boyd was safely transported, admitted to the hospital and receiving treatment—was Susannah Holiday.

She was a beautiful woman, with her athletic figure, dark, shoulder-length hair and blue-violet eyes, and Ian had felt an instant attraction to her. She'd been brave and compassionate, investigating when she spotted the runaway horse, finding the injured boy and calling for help, sticking around until it arrived.

Ian's years of experience had taught him that many people wouldn't have wanted to get involved to the extent Susannah had, not necessarily because they were unkind, but because they were afraid.

A few would even have ignored the signs of trouble and passed right on by, telling themselves that someone else would make the call, administer necessary first aid, etc.

Yes, Susannah Holiday was different. Strong and smart and courageous.

According to Jim, she was in town to look after her sister, Becky Bennet, and niece, Ellie. Further testament of her good character, he supposed, but a woman like Susannah? Well, she would be married, or at least engaged, wouldn't she?

There was no telling. Ian tuned back in to his daughters' running commentary on their life in Florida.

For the rest of the drive, he concentrated on following rapid-fire girl talk.

It was hard to believe, Susannah reflected, that she'd been in Copper Ridge for a whole week, though she'd accomplished a lot since she'd arrived—her main computer, SUV and other necessary belongings had been delivered, and the rental car returned.

She'd visited a still-unresponsive Becky again, kept up with her web design projects, and acquired a small house to renovate and resell. Had Becky's things placed in storage, so that the landlord could let his niece and her husband move in.

It was a lot, even for someone with Susannah's natural energy.

That was probably why Ellie asked the question she did, that morning, as they cruised the aisles at Home Depot, shopping for necessary paints, tile and vinyl flooring, bathroom fixtures and cabinets—the works.

They would have to wait a few days for everything to arrive, except for the paints, brushes and tarps, which they'd loaded into the back of the SUV.

"Are you going to stay in Copper Ridge *for good*?" Ellie asked, as she and Susannah headed back to the renovation project, which was also their temporary residence, the small, rundown, but basically sturdy house Susannah had chosen to fix up and flip. "Is that why you bought the house?"

"I've told you, Ellie-girl—I'm staying until I'm not needed anymore," Susannah replied honestly, reaching over to rest a hand on Ellie's shoulder. "But for now, consider me a local. You and Nico and I are going to check out of the hotel today and move in here."

Ellie's eyes were large and worried. "What if we need you, like, *forever*? Mom and me, I mean."

The question nearly splintered Susannah's heart. "You won't," she replied.

Ellie looked unconvinced. She was thin, and the new clothes Susannah had bought for her looked as though they were a bit too big.

In fact, she reminded Susannah of a little bird forced out of the nest before her wings were strong enough to support her.

"Listen," Susannah said, giving Ellie what she hoped was a reassuring smile. "You're going to grow up to be a strong, smart and capable woman. You'll go to college, work in a field you love, and most likely get married, too, and have children of your own."

"What about Mom? Suppose she doesn't get better?"

"She *will* get better," Susannah insisted. "We have to believe that, Ellie. And help *her* to believe it, too."

"What good does believing do?"

"You'd be surprised," Susannah answered, with another smile.

"You're so strong," Ellie pointed out, in the tone of a lament. "Mom and I are a couple of Bad Luck Bessies. That's what Mom says."

Susannah's response was just short of steely. "That's absolutely not true!" she protested, and for a moment, her fingers tightened on the steering wheel. "It isn't about good or bad luck, Ellie—you can be the version of yourself you *choose* to be! You just have to decide, make a plan, and stick to it." She stopped, drew in a steadying breath. "It won't always be easy, but if you don't give up, you'll have a good life."

The girl's eyes welled. "We lived in a junky house, and Mom's been sick, on and off, for as long as I can remember. I get bullied at school because I don't have nice clothes and a phone and stuff, like the other kids. They called me 'loser' and they didn't invite me for sleepovers, because they said I have cooties."

Susannah sighed inwardly. It was no wonder Ellie doubted that she and her mom would ever live happy lives. Things had always been so hard for them.

"Frankly, I'm not convinced a kid your age even needs a phone," Susannah replied. "And you're *not* a loser unless you choose to believe what those mean kids say. They may have a lot of fancy stuff, and they may be popular now, but if they judge other people like that, *they're* the real losers. Trust me, in this life, what goes around, comes around."

Ellie didn't answer, at least, not verbally. She folded her arms and jutted out her chin.

She could be stubborn, like her mother.

Like her aunt.

"Mom says I should have a phone," the girl insisted, brow furrowed. She didn't seem to be aware of the tears trickling down her cheeks. "Because there are really bad people out there, and I might need a way to call for help sometime. She's mad at herself because she thinks she's bad, too. She said I deserve a better mom."

The words struck Susannah hard, wounded her to the soul.

If she hadn't been driving, she would have gathered Ellie into her arms and hugged her tightly.

"Sweetheart," she said, sadly earnest. "You have to trust me, all right? Your mother loves you with her whole heart, but she has problems, that's all. And we're going to do everything we can to help her get well." She paused, considering Ellie's remark about "bad people." The idea gave her chills. Was there an underlying threat that Becky had been hiding? Like the return of her nasty ex, for instance? "As for getting you a phone," Susannah went on, once she'd regained her composure, "we'll see."

Ellie looked at Susannah with a tear-streaked but hopeful face. "If something scary happened, I could text you the secret word, and you'd know I needed help. If I had my own phone, I mean."

That much was true. But there were drawbacks to the idea, too: online predators, for one thing, and various social media sites where bullies were ever-ready to destroy a person's self-esteem, or even cause them to end their lives.

"If I get you a phone, Ellie, you'll have strict rules to follow, and if you break those rules, awful things might happen, because the internet can be a very dangerous place."

Ellie brightened. Sniffled. "I know. But I'll be good, Aunt Susannah. I promise."

"All right," Susannah conceded, with some reluctance, "but remember, I'm pretty tech savvy, since I mostly earn my living working on computers. I'll be checking from time to time, kiddo, and if you're taking chances, I'm going to know it, and it will be a long, *long* time before you get another phone, at least from me. Got it?"

By then, Ellie was beaming, though her eyes were still red-rimmed and her cheeks were wet. Susannah could not remember seeing that much joy in the child's face before, and her heart broke all over again.

"Let's go, then," she said, wrapping one arm around Ellie's shoulders and drawing her close against her side for a long moment. "We can unload the paint and other stuff later."

"*Yes!*" Ellie cried, and punched the air with one fist.

Although she strongly suspected she was being bamboozled, Susannah felt happy, too, if only because *Ellie* was happy.

Once they got home, she would waste no time setting up security features on the new device.

Meanwhile, Susannah reinforced her intention to help both Becky and Ellie, no matter what it took.

On the way to the mall on the edge of town, they met an ambulance, traveling at a normal speed, with no lights and no blaring siren.

Susannah leaned forward over the wheel and squinted, trying to identify either the driver or the person riding shotgun as Ian McKenzie, the paramedic she'd encountered on her very first day in the area. Although she couldn't have explained it, he'd been slipping in and out of her mind ever since that oh-so-brief encounter.

She'd even googled him a few times, out of simple curiosity— or so she told herself. He was divorced, with two stepchildren, and when he wasn't saving people from certain death, he was tending and training rescued horses on his nearby ranch.

Did he have a girlfriend?

It would be weird if he didn't. He was handsome, in a rugged sort of way, and for all practical intents and purposes, he was a hero.

And yet . . .

And yet *what*? She was letting her imagination run away with her.

"Aunt Susannah?"

Ellie's voice snapped her out of her ruminations, and she felt like an idiot, trying to find meaning in the way he'd smiled at her, or the single glance she and Ian had exchanged on the roadside.

"Yes?" she asked cheerfully.

"Can we please get something to eat at Manuel's after we buy the phone? I'm starving, and Manuel's has the best chicken enchiladas *ever*."

Susannah laughed, relieved to have her thoughts diverted from Ian McKenzie.

"Why not?" she answered.

Before they reached the phone store, however, the paramedic was back in her mind and taking up way too much space.

Why was she fixating on this guy? Did she really think anything could come of a chance meeting like theirs?

Get real, Susannah told herself. *Things like that only happen in rom-coms and romance novels.*

And it wasn't as though she was any kind of authority on love, after all. Her own romantic history was bland and boring. She'd dated in high school and college and, of course, since then, but she'd never met a man she felt passionate about.

She wasn't too picky, like some of her friends claimed; she knew what she wanted in a forever guy, and she wasn't going to settle, just to have a ring on her finger and a warm body to share her bed.

Fortunately, by the time these reflections on her personal preferences were getting to be too much, she was parking her SUV in front of the phone store.

With Susannah overseeing the process very carefully, Ellie chose a pink phone, apparently designed especially for kids whose parents or guardians wanted to limit cyber adventures to texting family and friends, watching approved videos, and using educational apps.

Susannah flashed her ATM card, and the purchase was official.

She and Ellie immediately exchanged contact information.

"This is *so* cool!" Ellie crowed, delighted.

"Definitely," Susannah admitted. "Now, let's head for Manuel's for an early supper."

The small restaurant was nearby, decorated festively, and lively with Mexican music. The smell of the food was so delectable that Susannah nearly swayed on her feet.

She and Ellie were seated quickly at a patio table encircled by wrought iron chairs. Colored lights blinked overhead, and the scents were even more pleasing there, since the kitchen adjoined the enclosed area.

Susannah craved a glass of red wine, preferably Shiraz, but she never drank when she knew she would have to drive. She'd have some after she and Ellie were back at the flip-house, where Nico awaited them, along with all the DIY projects involved in preparing a home for resale.

On top of that, she would need to visit Becky regularly, keep up with her web-design business, look after Ellie. And, although she was an accomplished multitasker, Susannah was nearly overwhelmed by all the stuff on her mental to-do list.

Ellie, meanwhile, was absorbed in her phone, and Susannah didn't protest.

The kid was happy, maybe for the first time in months, if not years.

For now, that was enough.

The preliminary corn chips, salsa and an especially tasty bean dip were delivered to their table quickly, and their orders were taken. Chicken enchiladas for Ellie, a taco salad for Susannah.

She was munching away on a chip loaded with said bean dip when, out of nowhere, *he* showed up, Ian McKenzie, clad in jeans, a T-shirt and scuffed boots, and flanked by two of the cutest little girls she'd ever seen.

"We meet again," he said, with a smile and a nod of his head.

"Hi, Mr. McKenzie," Ellie piped up, looking up from her phone at last and beaming with recognition. "Hi, Vivian and Mabel."

Vivian and Mabel? Seriously? Did people still give their children such old-fashioned names in this day and age?

"Hi, Ellie," the twins said, in what might have been one voice. They were exact duplicates of each other, and Susannah wondered if even Ian could tell them apart.

Surely he could, being their father, but she wondered how.

Caught off guard, Susannah muttered, "Ummm—hi there."

The three girls were chattering, catching up. Clearly, they were good friends, though Susannah had no idea when they'd met.

It was a lot to sort out. And when Ian broadened that sexy, knowing grin of his, she felt as though her chair was about to tip over backwards.

"Sit with us!" Ellie cried jubilantly.

Ian, still watching Susannah, arched one eyebrow in question.

"Er—yes, of course—let's sit together," she murmured.

Gleefully, the twins hauled back their chairs and sat down.

Ian sat opposite Susannah, amusement dancing in his eyes. He'd obviously picked up on her nervousness.

Behind her anxiety was a certain quiet joy that they were sitting at the same table; she hadn't expected to run into him again, not like this.

"I hope we're not intruding," he told her, as the waiter handed him a menu.

The remark made Susannah's cheeks pulse with heat. "No—no, you're perfectly welcome."

"Good," he responded.

And so began an evening that was, for Susannah, at once delightfully ordinary and strangely magical.

Chapter 4

That night, Ian's mind was full of Susannah Holiday; they'd had a long and pleasant conversation there on the patio at Manuel's, during dinner, and she'd supplied a few answers to questions he hadn't known how to ask.

She was single, an obvious plus. Never married, no kids. In town to see her sister and niece through a rough patch. She ran a web design business online and flipped houses as a sideline, doing much of the work herself, though she hired contractors for bigger jobs, like replacing roofs or upgrading the electrical systems and plumbing.

Susannah was successful by any definition of the word, and definitely ambitious, but she wasn't, well, *driven*. Even with a seemingly inexhaustible source of physical and mental energy, there was an undercurrent of deep serenity about her.

Of course, all that could be a façade, but Ian's instincts told him that Susannah was exactly who she appeared to be: the kind of person who would stop at the scene of an accident, as she had when Tim Boyd was hurt, and look after the kid *and* his frightened horse, standing by until help came. The kind who would drop everything, leave her busy life in Chicago without looking back and rush to a nothing-special town in northern Arizona to look after her struggling sister and young niece.

The sound of his daughters laughing in the bathroom down the hall—they were in their pajamas and brushing their teeth—brought Ian back to the present moment. Mostly.

He was standing on the threshold of the room Mabel and Vivian shared, with a large, empty garbage bag in one hand.

It had been three days since the twins arrived in Arizona—three *busy* days, tending the rescued mares, taking long horseback rides, living on takeout food and watching Disney and Pixar movies on TV at night. Hence, the room was a mess.

Multicolored balloons and twisted streamers drooped from the ceiling, and the floor was covered in wrapping paper and empty packages, both of which crunched under the soles of Ian's boots as he stepped inside and began to clean up.

Dub, having appointed himself as guardian, lay curled up on the rug between the girls' mismatched twin beds, watching Ian work.

As he collected the welcome-home decorations and gift packaging, Ian allowed his mind, once again, to wander back over the evening just past.

He definitely hadn't expected to encounter Susannah at Manuel's and, at first, the sight of her had taken him aback. Left him speechless, in fact.

He'd been grateful for the distraction Vivian and Mabel had created, spotting their summer friend, Ellie Bennet; it gave him a couple of moments to get back on track.

The three girls had met the summer before, during a barbecue at Jack and Harper O'Ballivan's ranch and, due to a shared love of horses and Saturday afternoon ballet lessons at the community center, they'd formed a bond.

Speaking of bonds, Ian reflected now, as his daughters reentered their bedroom like a pair of rockets fired from space, he'd felt a swift and powerful connection happen between himself and Susannah, silent but reverberating on impact.

Vivian and Mabel were now standing on their beds, jumping for joy, while Dub joined in by hopping back and forth between them, barking for all he was worth.

Ian sighed, smiled. On the inside, he was all a-jumble, happy to be with his daughters again, but unsettled, too. And more than a little confused.

Just as he was beginning to develop a headache, the twins simultaneously stopped jumping and landed, knees first, on their mattresses. Their eyes were huge as they focused on Ian's face.

"You like Susannah," Vivian told him. "*A lot.*"

"Right," Mabel agreed, with a note of sweet triumph.

Once again, Ian sighed. Shifting the now-bulging garbage bag to his left hand, he used his right to run his fingers through his hair.

"Of course I like her," he affirmed. "She's a nice person."

"She's *really* pretty," Vivian insisted.

"Yeah," agreed Mabel. "She is."

"And this conversation is headed—where?" he asked, with a smile. He was exhausted, but having his daughters around was a rare treat, and he didn't want to miss a moment.

"You need to get married again, like Mom did," Mabel said, taking the verbal lead this time. "It must be really lonely out here in the country when we're not around."

"It's true that I miss you when you're not here," Ian confirmed, choking up a little as he spoke, and hoping the girls hadn't noticed. They were kids, and he didn't want them worrying about him for any reason.

"I wish we could stay here all the time," Vivian confided.

That statement caused Ian to stash the garbage bag in the hall and then return to sit on the end of Vivian's bed, since Dub took up much of Mabel's.

"What do you mean by that?" he asked, once he'd recovered enough to speak.

At times, dealing with these bright, lively and outspoken children was like entering an emotional rodeo. Although he liked to think otherwise, there were issues, as there were in any divided family.

Earlier, the twins' exuberant delight had filled the room like a flood tide, but now, suddenly, it had receded, revealing the rocky ground beneath.

Mabel began to cry, so Ian reached across the gap between the beds and shifted her to sit next to him.

"Hey," Ian said softly. "What's the matter?"

Mabel ran the sleeve of her pajama top across her face and sniffled, bravely squaring her shoulders. "I'm scared," she confessed.

"Of what, sweetheart?" Ian's tone was cautious.

This was a new and disturbing development.

Why hadn't he picked up on the fact that something was wrong?

"We're both scared," Vivian added. "We're worried that you'll get married again, like Mom did, and then you and your wife will have babies and you won't want to be with us anymore."

With some maneuvering, Ian was able to shift around until he had one arm around Mabel, and the other around Vivian. Several moments passed, though, before he could answer; his mind was racing, and he didn't want to cry in front of his daughters.

His daughters? Biologically, they belonged to Catherine, and he was able to spend time with them only because she'd agreed to share custody. If his ex, or her new husband, decided to revoke that arrangement, there would be nothing Ian could do about it. When it came to these children, he had no legal rights whatsoever.

Technically, he wasn't even their stepfather anymore, now that Catherine had gotten married again.

Though he mostly kept this realization at bay, pressing it back whenever it arose to torment him, now it was looming over him like a dark specter.

Desperate, Ian latched on to the first truth that came to mind. "I love you both with all that I have and all that I am," he said. Then he followed up with the *second* truth: "And no matter what happens, I'll be there for you."

By then, their little arms were wrapped around his neck, and he felt their wet faces pressed against either side of his own.

"We want to stay with you," Vivian reiterated, clinging to him.

"Forever," Mabel all but wailed.

He waited for them to calm down a little.

Dub, whimpering with canine concern, paced the narrow space between the beds.

"What about your mom?" Ian asked gruffly, after two or three miserable minutes had gone by. "She loves you. She's a very good mother. Wouldn't you miss her if you came to live with me?"

"She has Tony now," Mabel murmured.

"She goes on a lot of trips," Vivian added, in the tone of a lament.

"And Tony has four kids. They're around almost every weekend."

Tony. The new husband.

As a precaution, Ian had run a background check on the man soon after Catherine had told him she'd met The One.

He hadn't been motivated by jealousy or anger; any romantic attachment he and Catherine had shared was long gone by then. He'd wanted to find out what kind of person Tony Delgotto was because he'd be sharing a home with Mabel and Vivian.

No other reason.

And the report on Delgotto had been clean. He was an airline pilot by profession, he'd served in the Air Force after getting a degree in aeronautics, married his college sweetheart, and fathered four children, two boys and two girls. Tragically, his wife had died of pancreatic cancer three years ago, and because as a pilot he traveled almost nonstop, the kids lived mostly with their grandparents.

The man's reputation was solid, both personally and professionally.

Not that Ian could have done a whole hell of a lot about it if he'd turned out to be a creep.

Anyway, Catherine was nobody's fool, nor was she the type to overlook red flags in any relationship. He still respected her very much.

"Look," Ian began, after clearing his throat, "it's always hard when the shape of a family changes. I understand that, and I'm sure your mom does, too."

"We wanted Mom to get married to you again, so we could all be together, like before," Vivian said. "That isn't going to happen, is it?"

"No," Ian managed, with much effort. "That isn't going to happen. Your mom and I are friends, but we don't love each other. Not the way a married couple ought to."

Vivian pulled away first, then Mabel.

Ian averted his gaze, blinking rapidly in the gathering darkness.

Dub stood still now, but he kept turning his head to look at one twin, then the other.

"Why not?" one of the girls asked, very softly. Ian couldn't have said which, because they not only looked alike, they sounded alike. And none of them had bothered to switch on a lamp, so the room was dim and shadowy.

Before he could respond, the other twin piped up. "Why don't you love Mom anymore? She's really pretty, and she's smart, and she's nice, too."

"She's all those things and more," Ian agreed, while his heart shattered into pieces, like an upended jigsaw puzzle, and tumbled down and down, into some inner abyss. "Things happened—we wanted different things, we were headed in different directions. It's grown-up stuff, and it's hard to explain. We both love you deeply—that's what's important."

"But you text her all the time, and she texts you," Vivian insisted, lying down now and pulling her covers up to her chin. Mabel did the same.

Still fretful, Dub gave a soft whimper, and Ian reached out to ruffle the dog's ears.

"Those texts are mostly about the two of you," Ian said. "The phone calls, too."

"Okay," chorused his beloved daughters.

"What about Tony?" he heard himself ask. He hadn't planned to bring up Catherine's new husband; the words just slipped out, so he went on. "Do you like him?"

Just then, a silvery splash of moonlight spilled in through the window above the beds, briefly illuminating the children's faces.

"He's all right," Mabel conceded.

"He's always kissing Mom," Vivian elaborated. "Even when we're right there."

Ian chuckled, relieved. "That's normal, kiddos. He and your mom are in love, after all. And they're married."

Neither twin offered a confirmation—or a denial.

They'd had a long day, and soon they'd be asleep.

For now, any further discussion would have to wait.

Ian tucked them in, kissed their foreheads, and reminded them to say their prayers.

Dub slumped down on the rug with a huff of a sigh, and Ian

left the room, leaving the door open just far enough to let the dog pass through if he wanted.

In the clean but outdated kitchen, Ian brewed a cup of coffee and gazed out of the window over the sink.

Memories washed over him, in gentle but poignant waves.

His grandmother, Dora, kneading bread dough and listening to music on an old-fashioned portable radio.

His grandfather, Jeb, stomping snow off his feet on the back step before lugging in yet another armload of wood for the stove in the living room.

His childhood self, playing on the floor—a middle-schooler, struggling with homework—a teenager, sorting through a variety of dreams for his future.

Those people, this house, this land—he was part of the place, and it was part of him. In fact, he drew much of his strength from just being there, under those spectacular skies.

Sipping his coffee, Ian took his phone from the countertop, where it had been charging, and sat down at the table.

It was late in Arizona, even later in Miami.

Ian scrolled earlier exchanges with Catherine anyway, then tapped in a brief text message.

We need to talk.

She didn't respond until the following morning, when he and the girls were gathered around the kitchen table, filling up on bacon, eggs and fried potatoes.

Ian's phone chimed and he looked down at it, saw that there was a text from Catherine, and tapped in.

That sounds serious, she'd written. **What's going on out there?**

Being modern kids, Vivian and Mabel barely noticed that Ian was focused on his phone; they were both trying to sneak bits of bacon to Dub, who was under the table, and chattering away about an upcoming trip to town.

There was no sign of last night's upset. Not yet, anyway.

First of all, don't panic, Ian replied. **The girls are fine; there's nothing to worry about.** But this is too complicated for texting, so I'm hoping we can arrange a time to actually talk. A Zoom call, maybe, when Vivian and Mabel are watching *Frozen* for the hundredth time?

Catherine responded quickly. **How about** *now,* **Ian?** *Something* **must be up, and I need to know what it is.**

Sorry, he tapped in. **The kids are right here, and I don't want them listening in.**

Ian!

Catherine, calm down. I told you there was nothing to worry about.

The phone rang in his hand.

Ian sighed, shoved back his chair, muttered an excuse to the twins, and left the room, shutting himself away in his home office.

He greeted his ex-wife in a terse undertone. "*Damn* it, Catherine. This isn't the time—"

"Oh, yes, it is," Catherine shot back. "Talk to me, Ian. I'm freaking out here!"

"Listen," Ian began, his voice even now, and barely above a whisper. "You need to get a grip. Like I said, we can discuss this later."

"*Ian.*" Catherine paused, sucked in angry breath. "If you want to talk, it must be about the girls. I'm their mother and I want you to tell me what's wrong—*now.*"

Ian sank into his desk chair and shut his eyes, barely managing to suppress a heavy sigh. Catherine was in mother-hen mode; she wouldn't be put off.

And as frustrating as that was, he couldn't really blame her.

"You're not going to like this," he warned, listening for footsteps in the hallway outside his office. He didn't want the twins overhearing what he had to say.

"I'd already guessed that much," Catherine snapped. *"Talk."*

Ian drew a deep breath, released it slowly and answered. "It's about the twins, Cath. I need to know that everything is okay when they're with you and Tony."

"What on earth have they told you?"

"You're going to have to ask them about that."

"Then why in *hell* did you text me in the first place?" Catherine's demand was justified. The conversation was going nowhere good; maybe he should have given the matter a little more thought before stirring the pot like this.

On the other hand, it wouldn't be right to keep this particular worry to himself. Catherine was a fantastic mother, and he'd never kept things from her, at least not when those things concerned the twins.

"Will you chill a little?" he asked.

"I'm calling the girls *right now!*" Catherine sputtered.

Then she ended the call.

Damn, Ian thought. Could he have handled the exchange any worse?

After that, Ian went back to the kitchen, leaned against the counter with his arms folded, and waited. Vivian and Mabel, still at the table, were dressed to go riding, but they were playing games on their phones.

Vivian's rang, and she paused the game to see who was calling.

"It's Mom," she said, then, "Hello?"

"Put the phone on speaker, Vivian, so you and your sister can both hear what I have to say," Catherine instructed, and her voice was loud enough that Ian heard her clearly. She sounded controlled. Stiff.

Vivian obeyed, and Mabel moved her chair closer to her sister's.

"Your dad seems to think there's a problem," Catherine

said. She wasn't exactly ranting, but she was clearly troubled. "Would you girls like to tell me what it is?"

The girls looked at each other, then Ian.

Vivian did not hesitate to reply. "It's not actually a problem," she said, and she might have been a no-nonsense woman, rather than a child, she was that forthright. "Mabel and me— we'd like to stay here with Dad. Go to school in Copper Ridge and everything."

Catherine must have been stunned to silence, because she said nothing in response.

"Mom?" Mabel prompted, leaning in so close to Vivian's phone that she might as well have crawled onto the tabletop. "Did you faint or something?"

"No—no," Catherine answered, at some length. "I'm just surprised, that's all. I thought everything was going pretty well—you like Tony, right? And his kids, too?"

"Tony's nice," Vivian replied, in the same matter-of-fact tone she'd used before. She was certainly her mother's daughter. "But he's not Dad."

"I see," Catherine said, though it was obvious, at least to Ian, that she didn't see at all. She was confounded, stunned, and Ian felt sorry for her.

"We love you a lot, Mom," Mabel interjected.

"I love you and your sister," Catherine answered. "But this is something we need to talk about in person—you and Mabel, your dad, and me." A pause followed, during which Ian felt oddly tense, and inwardly he braced himself. Then, finally, the other shoe dropped. "I'm coming out there—as soon as I've booked my flight and arranged for some time off, I'll be on my way."

Ian closed his eyes.

Chances were good that he was about to lose the daughters of his heart.

If he knew Catherine, she would listen to everything the

girls had to say about staying with him, then help them pack for the trip back home to Miami.

In fact, he might not see them again for years, if ever.

They would miss him for a while, but they'd grow and change as time went by, and he wouldn't be "Dad" anymore.

In Catherine's view, that title probably belonged to Tony now.

For his daughters' sake, Ian reflected, still leaning against the kitchen counter, he was going to have to let go.

Chapter 5

In towns the size of Copper Ridge, Arizona, word really *does* get around fast.

No more than fifteen minutes after Ian McKenzie's ex-wife, Catherine, sped straight through town in a rental car, clearly headed for his ranch, half the county knew something was up. And that included Susannah. She happened to be in the Cool Beans Coffee Shop on Main Street that evening, when Piper Harrington, a waitress from a café down the street, came rushing in, bursting with the news.

A collective gasp rose from the general population, and a few people actually rushed to the windows.

Susannah frowned. Until the young woman's breathless announcement, she'd been calmly sipping an iced mocha latte and, using her laptop, putting the finishing touches to a website she'd been working on for weeks. It was a huge project, and the final payment, due on the client's approval, would be enough to cover her and Ellie's living costs for a long time.

Her plan was to take a few months off from her web-design work, passing the most urgent projects on to other small companies; she would limit her work to fixing up the flip house for resale.

Her primary objective, naturally, was to be more available to her sister and her niece as long as they needed her help.

And it looked like that would be a while—though, according to a call from Dr. Mowgat that morning, Becky was beginning to respond to treatment. As encouraging as that news had been, it was plain to everyone that her full recovery might be a long time coming—if it came at all.

All those concerns were pushed to one side, however, as Susannah took in Piper's announcement and sorted through it mentally, in her usual methodical way. Ian's former wife was in town. What did that mean?

It's none of your business, Susannah informed herself silently.

Just the same, she felt as though a trap door had just sprung open beneath her feet, leaving her dangling over a dark hole. She actually gripped the sides of the glass tabletop, the plummeting sensation was that strong.

Get a grip, warned the ever-practical voice in her head. *Maybe you had a great time with Ian and the kids last night at Manuel's, and maybe you're attracted to the man, but you have no claim on him, none whatsoever.*

She felt herself flush.

A few deep breaths restored her equanimity, if not her calm mindset.

Why did Piper, or any of these people, think it was okay to spread gossip like this? The waitress had been downright *exuberant* about it, for Pete's sake.

Really—who did that?

Small-town folks, it would seem. Once again, and for only a few moments, Susannah sincerely wished she'd taken Ellie to stay with her at her place in Chicago instead of relocating to Copper Ridge. She could have flown back and forth between there and Flagstaff to visit Becky and avoided this kind of drama.

You're not being fair, judging a whole town like that, her inner self pointed out.

That was true.

Chagrined, Susannah sighed, closed her laptop, began gathering her belongings—several notebooks, colored markers, and sketches of features she was suggesting for the website she'd been building, pixel by pixel, or so it seemed.

"Don't pay too much attention to the fuss," a female voice advised. A voice *outside* Susannah's head this time. "Some people around here have too much free time, and Piper, in particular, thrives on the least hint of drama."

She turned and saw Mrs. Norman, the local librarian, standing nearby, one wrinkled and beringed hand resting gently on Ellie's left shoulder. Susannah had met the woman that afternoon, when she'd dropped Ellie off for a meeting of the Tween-Scene Book Club, and taken an immediate liking to her.

Belatedly, Susannah acknowledged Mrs. Norman with a slight smile and a nod, but her focus had already shifted to Ellie, who looked upset.

"What's wrong, honey?" she asked, cupping one hand under Ellie's chin and lifting so she could look into the girl's moist blue eyes.

"Molly Armstrong said my mom is in a lunatic asylum because she's insane," Ellie admitted. "Some of the other kids thought that was funny and they started moving around like zombies, making stupid faces and stuff. They laughed at me and said I'll probably be put away soon, too, just like Mom."

Hot rage jolted through Susannah's system. She was glad those cruel children weren't standing in front of her now, because she wasn't entirely sure she could have contained her fury. The urge to set the little monsters straight was like consuming fire.

She concentrated on her breathing.

In. Out. In. Out.

Just breathe.

While Susannah was trying to quell her anger, Mrs. Norman was shaking her gray head. "As old as I am, I still don't understand why anyone would treat another person so badly. It's entirely unacceptable."

Susannah hugged Ellie tight, then turned her attention back to the librarian. "More bullying," she mused. "And in a public library, no less."

Mrs. Norman straightened her shoulders, and her smile, though wobbly, seemed genuinely sympathetic. "If only I'd been there when the incident began—I had to leave the room for a few minutes to take an important telephone call," she explained. "When I came back and found those girls behaving so cruelly, I sent them all straight home and told them they couldn't participate in the book club again until I'd spoken to their parents. Apologies will be forthcoming, if I have anything to say about it."

Susannah nodded glumly, squeezed Ellie once more, then released her. "Thank you," she said, very quietly. She couldn't have asked the librarian for the parents' contact info, that would have been unethical, but she intended to track down each and every one of them and let them know what she thought of their daughters' reprehensible actions.

Once again, as she and Ellie headed for the exit, followed by Mrs. Norman, Susannah questioned her decision to come to Copper Ridge instead of collecting Ellie and taking her back to Chicago.

Twenty minutes later, back in the chaotic comfort of their present residence, the flip house, Ellie gathered Nico into her arms, buried her face in his fur, and collapsed onto the second-hand couch Susannah had purchased a few days before, at an estate sale.

"Why do people hate me, Aunt Susannah?" Ellie asked plaintively, her voice muffled by Nico's soft, purring body.

Susannah set her laptop, notebooks, etc., on top of the upended cardboard box serving as a coffee table and plunked herself down alongside Ellie, slipping an arm around the girl's shoulders, momentarily stuck for an answer. After all, she herself didn't understand what motivated some people to bully others.

Nico gave a long meow and snuggled against Ellie's flat little chest.

"I don't think anyone really hates you, sweetheart," Susannah replied, after several long moments of thought. "People can be messed up for all kinds of reasons, and bullies, especially, are usually cowards, deep down. They're afraid, or angry with someone, often themselves, so they project their feelings onto others."

"What are they scared of?" Ellie asked, with a puzzled frown.

"All kinds of things, probably," Susannah responded with a shrug and a soft sigh. "But here's the important thing to remember: You can't allow other people's opinions to determine what you think about *yourself*. *You* get to decide what kind of person you want to be, no one else."

"Is that why you always seem to know what to do when something bad happens?"

Susannah leaned in a little, stroked Nico's silky back with a light hand as she considered her answer. "I have problems, just like everyone else, Ellie. And you need to remember that there are actually *lots* of people who like you. Vivian and Mabel, for instance."

The mention of the twins brought Ian to mind and, with him, the return of his ex-wife. Although she hadn't seen the former Mrs. McKenzie speeding along Main Street, the murmurings of some of the other customers in the coffee shop had clued her in that the woman must have been angry, if she was driving recklessly.

Suddenly, Ellie smiled, bringing Susannah back into the flow of their conversation. The girl kissed the top of Nico's head and said, "They want me to come out to the ranch to ride horses with them."

"The twins have horses of their own?" Susannah asked, still a little distracted.

Of course that wasn't major news. The girls' father owned a ranch. He worked with horses, when he wasn't serving as a paramedic.

Briefly, a memory of Tim Boyd's accident and the fitful gelding flashed into her mind. Inevitably, she thought of Ian again, not as the twins' dad, but as the quiet, confident man she'd met that day. Having supper with him and his children at Manuel's had underscored those impressions.

Meanwhile, Ellie was nodding, her face eager. "Ponies. Vivian and Mabel each have one of their very own."

"That's exciting," Susannah muttered, thrown off balance again.

That happened whenever Ian's image popped into her mind, which was often. Once again, she had to scramble a little to get back to the present moment.

"Someday I'm going to have a horse, too," Ellie announced, with a lift of her elegant little chin. When she grew up, she was going to be every bit as lovely as her mother.

But stable, happy and productive.

Please, God.

"That's an excellent goal," Susannah replied, relieved that Ellie's thoughts had taken a positive turn. There needed to be more of that. "If I remember correctly, you enjoy ballet classes at the community center, too."

"That's where I met Vivian and Mabel," Ellie confirmed. "That was last summer, when they were visiting their dad. It was a lot of fun, but I'm too old now to be in the same dance class as them." That last part seemed to sadden the child a little, though she was in a much better mood than before. "They're only nine, and I'm already twelve."

"Maybe you'll be in different classes," Susannah said, "but they'll still be your friends. And you can make new ones, too, of course. Taking a class or joining a group is a good way to do that."

"Do you have a lot of friends, Aunt Susannah?"

Susannah hesitated, but only for a moment. "Yes," she said. "Some I met in college, and some I met through work, before and after I started my business. There are others from a theatre group I joined for a while, and a gardening club—things like that."

"Were people mean to you when you were my age?"

Again, she hesitated. "No," she said.

"Did Mom have lots of friends back then? When both of you were kids?"

Oh, boy.

Susannah drew a deep breath, let it out again, very slowly. "Your mom is my big sister, and when we were young—even younger than you are now—she had lots of friends. She was funny and mischievous and sweet and everyone liked her."

"But then—?" Ellie's expression was somber again. She held Nico a little closer, and he squirmed a bit, so she released her hold on him. "Things changed, didn't they?"

Susannah bit her lower lip, then replied, "Something bad happened to your mom when she was thirteen. She would never tell anyone what it was—not even our parents, or her doctors, or the pastor of our church."

Ellie's pale eyebrows drew together for a second or so, as she tried to understand.

Her response, when it finally came, startled Susannah.

"She has really horrible nightmares sometimes. When that

happens, she screams and cries. A few times, she made me hide in the coat closet, or downstairs in the basement, behind the furnace. She thought somebody was after us."

Susannah was cautious. She couldn't afford to go rushing in with a lot of specific questions; that might spook Ellie into silence. Like it had always done with Becky.

"Really?" she asked, almost in a whisper.

Ellie nodded. "Most times, she wakes herself up with all that screaming, and then she can't go back to sleep."

"Did she ever tell you what her nightmares were about?"

Ellie shook her head. "I asked her lots of times, but she said I was too young to be burdened with a lot of bad thoughts."

Susannah understood, of course she did.

Ellie was still a child, after all.

"I wish I knew what frightens her so much," Susannah said thoughtfully, more to herself than Ellie. "Maybe then I could really help her."

Ellie was quiet for a long time, clearly wandering through a maze of memories, all of them sad and scary. What a toll Becky's mental illness had taken—*was taking*—on this innocent girl.

It was so frustrating.

In the next moment, Ellie startled Susannah all over again.

"Mom used to write stuff in those little notebooks—the kind they sell at Dollar Tree. She kept them hidden, though, so I never got to read any of them."

Susannah nearly bolted to her feet.

Becky kept journals?

She'd never known that. Although she was intelligent, Becky wasn't much for reading *or* writing; when she was in a good place mentally, she watched movies on Hallmark and Lifetime. She bowled and went dancing, wore makeup and did up her hair.

Susannah's heart ached, but learning that Becky must have recorded at least a few of her bad dreams, and some of her waking feelings and struggles as well, gave her a rush of hope.

"Do you know where the notebooks are now?" she asked carefully.

Ellie's answer—a shake of her head—was what Susannah had expected, but she still felt a buzz of excitement. She *had* to find those notebooks; they might well be the key to reaching Becky, convincing her that sharing whatever trauma she had experienced, however horrible it might have been, might lead to a turning point.

If it wasn't for the secret she was harboring, Becky could begin the healing process, at long last, and build new lives for herself and for Ellie.

Tears sprang to Susannah's eyes, and she turned, looked away. Then, deciding that hiding things from Ellie was unfair, and might do more harm than good, she met her niece's concerned, curious gaze.

"What's wrong, Aunt Susannah?" the child asked, in a near whisper. By that time, Nico had jumped down from her lap and wandered into the kitchen, probably heading for his food and water bowls.

"All this trouble, it breaks my heart. I love you and your mom so much," Susannah said frankly. "With Mom and Dad— Gramma and Grampa—both gone, you and Becky are all the family I have. And more than anything in the world, I want you both to be safe and happy."

Ellie tipped sideways and rested her head against Susannah's shoulder. "Grampa Jake wasn't Mom's dad, huh? He was yours."

Yet again, Susannah had to reorient herself.

"That's right," she said. "Your mom's father was Michael Bennet. He died when she was only about six months old. Your grandmother—my mom—married my dad, John Holiday, around a year and a half after she became a widow. I was born when Becky was three."

Ellie nodded. She'd been told that part of the story before, of course, but she seemed to like hearing it anyway.

"I miss Gramma and Grampa," she said.

Susannah gave her a one-armed hug. Stella and John Holiday had died of severe cases of Covid during the pandemic, only a month apart, and a day didn't go by when Susannah didn't wish she could see them again, hear their voices, hug them and be hugged in return.

They'd been excellent parents, both of them, and John Holiday had loved his stepdaughter, Becky, as much as he'd loved Susannah. And they'd both adored Ellie, their only grandchild.

The loss of them had been devastating for all concerned — especially Becky.

Susannah steered her thoughts back to the notebooks Ellie had just mentioned. Had Becky kept them, or thrown them away, during one of her bouts of depression?

There was only one way to find out, and that was by entering the storage unit where Susannah had had her things stored after Becky's landlord decided the ramshackle little house had to be emptied so that his niece and her family could move in, and going through every single box and bag in search of her sister's journals.

If she found them, it might change everything.

The odds were against her, but that was nothing new.

She intended to forge ahead, no matter what.

Chapter 6

Catherine arrived at the ranch that same evening, as she'd said she would, red-gray clouds billowing all around the rental car as she tapped on the brakes and peered curiously at Ian through the windshield.

Ian was mildly amused, watching her sit stiffly behind the wheel as she waited for the dust to settle.

Dub, probably thrilled to have another visitor, any visitor, barked an ear-splitting welcome.

"Mom!" the twins cried, in typical harmony. They'd been sitting on the top rail of the corral fence, watching as Ian worked with the nervous little rescue mare he'd named Ragamuffin.

They jumped down and raced toward the car to greet their mother when she finally emerged, looking as beautiful as ever, with her chin-length blonde hair and trim, fit figure. She was wearing a black designer pantsuit, fancy sandals and just the right amount of gold jewelry.

Catherine had always been classy.

Watching as Vivian and Mabel mobbed their mother with

hugs, Ian felt a combination of joy and sorrow—joy because the girls were obviously happy, and sorrow for the loss of his family.

The twins took Catherine's hands and pulled her in Ian's direction.

He smiled, nodded a greeting, and waited.

Catherine ran her gaze over him, taking in his cotton work shirt, worn jeans, even his boots.

"You look good," she told him.

"So do you," Ian replied honestly. His attraction to her had long since vanished, but she *was* a fine-looking woman. Strangely, though, even with Catherine standing right in front of him, evoking all sorts of memories, Susannah Holiday popped into his mind.

Ever since their impromptu dinner together at Manuel's, he'd been focused on asking her out, but now definitely wasn't the time to be thinking of things like that.

This could be the end of his time with the girls, for one thing.

There was too much at stake; he couldn't let his thoughts wander.

"You're happy?" Catherine asked quietly, and he knew she cared about the answer and about him, if not in a romantic way.

"Happy enough," he answered, with a half smile.

Sunset was spilling colorfully across the eastern sky by then, turning parts of it from lavender to purple, others from light red to deep crimson, all with a current of blue streaming across the mountaintops. In an hour or so, it would be dark and the stars would come out, bright as sequins, dancing around a pale cycle of the moon.

Ian felt the familiar sense of connection with the land, and that was a comfort to him.

"You hungry?" he asked, when Catherine didn't speak.

"Sort of," she admitted, with a faltering smile. Dub had calmed down by then, but he was rubbing against her legs, no doubt shedding hair all over the legs of her elegant pantsuit. "It's been a long day, and I couldn't eat much on the plane." She draped an arm around each of the girls' shoulders and held them close against her sides, though the move was gentle and affectionate, rather than possessive. "Suppose we all go to town and have dinner somewhere nice? I'm buying."

Vivian beamed up at her mom, shook her head and said, "We've got a big pot of beef stew simmering on the stove, so supper's covered."

Briefly, Catherine's and Ian's gazes connected, then swung away from each other.

"And Dad got the fold-out bed ready, too," Mabel put in, as if she'd read his mind. "Clean sheets and everything. We even aired out the comforter on the clothesline."

Catherine's cheeks pinkened slightly and she looked a little off-kilter. "Well—"

Ian smiled. "It's okay," he assured her, as the twins suddenly bolted for the car, where they promptly fetched Catherine's very small suitcase and handbag. Since the kids were well out of earshot, he added, "I can control my animal instincts, Cath, and I won't be bothering you. You know that."

Nervously, Catherine laughed. "I do know that," she replied. "Anyway, I want to be near my children."

The twins were playing porter, hauling their mother's belongings into the house.

"They love you, Catherine," Ian felt compelled to remind her.

"But they want to stay with you," Catherine pointed out, somewhat sadly.

"It's your decision to make, no one else's," he said. "They're your daughters, after all."

Unexpectedly, tears formed in Catherine's lovely blue-green eyes. "They're yours, too, Ian," she said.

"You mean that?" Ian asked, hardly daring to hope.

"Of course I do. You're the only father they've ever known. Tony's a good man, and I think the girls like him, but he could never replace you, not in their eyes anyway. I suspect, in fact, that my husband's got his hands full, between his own four children, his job and a new marriage, so adding step-parenting to all that might be a struggle. Maybe we all need a bit of space, time to adjust and get our bearings."

"Maybe," Ian agreed quietly, and, laying a hand to the small of his ex-wife's back, he steered her gently in the direction of the house. "You're hungry and tired. For tonight, let's keep it simple. You'll feel stronger tomorrow—we can talk then."

"You're right," she answered wearily.

"Go on inside," he said. "Vivian and Mabel will be waiting, and I've got to get Ragamuffin and the other horses into the barn."

Catherine, almost to the door, turned her head to look at Ian and smiled. "*Ragamuffin?* Did you come up with that name?"

"Yep," Ian replied, with an answering smile. "She's had a rough time, and she needs special treatment."

"You haven't changed," Catherine said, her tone kind and soft. "You still can't pass up a stray." She glanced at Dub, who was hovering at Ian's side by then, ready, as always, to "help" with the chores. Like the horses, the dog was a rescue, and she knew that. "I wish there were more people like you in this chaotic world of ours."

Ian smiled again, but said nothing. Compliments always made him a little uncomfortable.

He was no saint, after all.

He just liked making a bad situation better, when and if he could.

As he settled the horses into their stalls for the night, filled their feeders with hay and a scoop of grain, Dub at his side the whole time, like always, Ian thought about his life.

He loved his daughters. He loved his horses and, of course, his dog.

As for his job, well, he couldn't imagine doing anything else for a living.

But there was no denying that he was lonely, specifically for the company of a woman.

A woman like Susannah, for instance.

He didn't know her very well—there hadn't been time for that, of course—but he'd thought about her plenty since that first encounter on the road between Flagstaff and Copper Ridge. She hadn't hesitated to push up her proverbial sleeves and wade right into the task at hand.

At Manuel's, while three little girls chattered and admired Ellie's new phone, he'd gotten the basics. Susannah was in Copper Ridge to take care of her sister and her niece, but the arrangement was temporary, she'd said so. She had friends and a condo and a *life* in Chicago, and she planned on going back when the time was right.

Getting close to her was more of an emotional risk than it would be with a local woman, he had to admit. Just as Catherine had chosen to leave Phoenix for Miami, back in the day, Susannah would eventually return to the Windy City as soon as Becky and Ellie were on their feet again, and able to make it on their own.

Or, she might simply take them with her when she left.

What Ian knew for sure about Susannah was that she wouldn't abandon her family, however complicated things might get, and what he knew about *himself* was that he wasn't leaving the ranch; he could no more do that than walk on water.

In fact, he intended to be buried in the small cemetery hidden away in a copse of trees on the other side of the property. His grandparents had been laid to rest there, along with his great-grandparents, and one day—hopefully far in the future— he would join them.

Taking all those things into consideration, he wondered if there was any point in asking Susannah out in the first place, getting his hopes up, and all that. She was a city girl, and he had to remember that. After Chicago, Copper Ridge had to seem pretty boring to her.

Recalling the break with Catherine, some of the old heartache returned in a rush.

Strong as he was, by nature and by decision, Ian didn't figure he could go through that kind of loss again and remain the person he was.

The first round had nearly killed him, after all.

Resigned, and somewhat saddened, Ian finished his chores and, with a sigh, latched the barn door.

Dub, so close Ian almost tripped over him, gave a sympathetic whimper.

Animals, he reflected, no matter what the skeptics said, could read emotions.

Ian ruffled Dub's ears and spoke gently to him, and they made their way through the gathering twilight toward the house.

Inside, the girls were waiting to greet Dub; they'd filled his water and food bowls, and they showered him with sweet verbal nonsense.

His tail, instead of wagging, spun a wide circle, counterclockwise, reminding Ian of a helicopter blade. One of these days, that three-legged mutt might just take off and fly around the room.

Ian nodded a hello to Catherine on his way to the bathroom sink, where he would wash up and swap out his work shirt for a clean one.

While he was outside tending the horses, Catherine had changed into jeans, a T-shirt and sneakers and tied her hair up into a ponytail. She smiled as he passed, and went on setting the table for supper.

The familiarity of the scene knotted Ian's throat and made the backs of his eyes sting. Before everything between him and Catherine had gone to hell in a handbasket, they'd shared homey evenings like this whenever possible—which wasn't all that often, actually, considering the demands of their jobs—and Ian had loved those times. Felt like part of a family again.

In the bathroom, he took off his shirt, tossed it into the hamper, and turned on the hot and cold water taps. He soaped up, rinsed, toweled himself almost dry, and made for his bedroom.

There, he took a blue sweatshirt from the chest of drawers and hauled it on over his head. He'd take a shower before he went to bed, but for the time being, he was clean enough to make an appearance at the table.

Upon his return to the kitchen, Ian found the girls already seated and scrolling through their phones. Without a word, or a confirmation from Catherine, he collected the devices and set them aside.

He half expected Vivian and Mabel to protest, but they didn't. They were all smiles as Catherine set steaming, fragrant bowls of stew in front of them, and the sight of them gave Ian another pang of sadness.

Were they hoping their parents would fall in love all over again, and remarry, so the four of them could live as a family? A stranger, viewing the Norman Rockwellian scene, would probably never guess the truth.

Ian waited until Catherine was seated, then sat down in his usual place at the end of the table. It was Mabel's turn to say grace, and what she said caused both adults to lock gazes. "Dear God, thank you for this food and thanks too that we're all together tonight, like a real family—Mom and Dad and me and Vivian." A pause. "And Dub. Amen."

After the amens, Ian tucked into his supper. He'd put in a long day, between the kids, the horses, and Catherine's arrival, and he was hungry enough, as his grandfather used to say, to eat the north end of a southbound skunk.

The twins chattered, as usual, telling their mother all about "helping" their dad work with the rescue horses, riding their ponies, and about their friend Ellie and her aunt, Susannah, who was very pretty and something of a local hero in the bargain, since she'd probably saved Tim Boyd's life after he got thrown from his horse. Not only that, but she was helping Ellie and her sick mom, too.

Catherine listened, smiled slightly, and met Ian's gaze.

He felt his neck heat up and looked away.

In a lot of ways, Catherine hadn't changed. She was very good at picking up on nuances and pursuing them until she got to the truth.

Natural enough, Ian reminded himself, feeling a bit cornered, given that she was a prosecuting attorney. A very successful one at that.

After supper, and having loaded the dishwasher, at their mom's insistence, Vivian and Mabel headed for the living room, closely followed by Dub.

Soon, the TV came on, spilling the opening overture of yet another Disney movie.

Ian and Catherine remained at the kitchen table, with cups of coffee steaming in front of them.

"Susannah, huh?" Catherine inquired lightly. "Do you realize you actually *blushed* when her name was mentioned a little while ago?"

Ian cleared his throat. "I've known her for less than a week, Catherine," he replied.

"Sometimes," Catherine answered, "a week is all the time two people need to know they belong together."

He expelled a skeptical breath, though not in a confrontational way. Catherine wasn't his enemy.

"Is that how it was for you and Tony?" he asked, teasing.

Her answer shouldn't have surprised him. "Yes," she told him. A fairly long pause followed, while Ian concentrated on stirring his black coffee and Catherine sipped thoughtfully from her cup. When she went on, the mood had lightened considerably. "It was wild, how quickly we fell in love and knew it was for real. If I'd read our story in a book, I wouldn't have believed it for a moment."

Ian's smile was genuine. "That's great, Catherine," he said.

"Ian," Catherine said, sounding both good-natured and serious, "I want you to be every bit as happy as I am. This place"— she gestured, meaning the ranch itself—"is beautiful, but you're lonely here. It must be really hard when the girls are with me, in Miami. You need to open your mind and your heart to opportunities to find the right person to spend the rest of your life with. We may be divorced, but you're a catch, Ian McKenzie— for real. So stop holding yourself prisoner and take some chances."

Ian absorbed Catherine's words, but he didn't continue the discussion. He could have said he took plenty of chances, especially as a sometime firefighter, or said he'd dated plenty of women since they'd parted, or made a dozen other excuses.

He'd have been tripped up by his own honesty in the process, because the truth was, Catherine was right.

He was one lonesome cowboy.

Chapter 7

After several hours spent searching through bags and boxes in the storage unit where Becky and Ellie's things were stashed, and being bitten by numerous mosquitos, Susannah finally struck it lucky.

Becky's notebooks, tattered and stained and bent, were stuffed into plastic shopping bags at the bottom of a tilting cardboard cube draped in cobwebs. Susannah had seen the box before, taped shut and obviously long forgotten, jammed into the dusty space under the basement steps at her sister's rented house.

She hadn't looked inside at the time; in fact, she'd almost left the thing behind.

Alas, after going through practically everything her sister and niece owned, the box had represented one last, flimsy hope that Becky's journals still existed. The chances were pretty high, after all, that she'd thrown them away or burned them to ashes long ago.

Ellie, worn out by nearly two hours of effort, now occupied a rusty-legged, sagging lawn chair near the raised door of the unit. She was scrolling through photographs on her phone.

Susannah let out a low cry of "*Yes!*" when, after digging through layers of rusted wire coat hangers, old newspapers, and T-shirts-turned-rags, she found the first supermarket bag and opened it.

There were at least a dozen small notebooks inside, multicolored, with faded covers and thumb-worn edges. The handwriting inside the first one she opened was definitely Becky's, though the paper was stained and the pencil lines barely visible.

She promptly decided to decipher the entries later, at home.

"What?" Ellie asked anxiously, bolting to her feet. "What happened?"

"I think I found them," Susannah replied, flipping through a second journal without registering the lines written inside. Again, the style, though childish, with its rounded, loopy letters and tiny circles dotting the *i*'s, was Becky's. "Your mom's notebooks, I mean."

"Wow," Ellie breathed. She was very tired—it was late, and she was just a kid—but the find had clearly shocked her back to wide-eyed alertness. "Do—do you think we should read them? Without asking Mom, I mean?"

"Under any other circumstances," Susannah answered quietly, "reading them would definitely be wrong. Journals and diaries are meant to be private. But this is a unique situation—a possible clue to what happened to your mom that set off her mental illness, way back when she was only a year older than you are now." She paused, fought back a sudden and unexpected rush of tears—tears of hope, tears of relief, tears of sorrow, because Becky's illness had all but ruined her life, and Ellie's, too. "Whatever it was, it's been causing her problems ever since, Ellie, and if there's something in these notebooks that explains things, we need to find it."

"And then what?" Ellie asked, sounding uncertain. Undoubtedly, Becky had warned her that the journals were strictly off-limits.

"And then we share the information with Becky's doctors. They'll almost surely be able to use it to help her get better—for real."

There might be reason to involve the police, too, though Susannah didn't mention that. Ellie's mother was in a mental hospital; the girl had enough to worry about without adding extra layers.

"What if it doesn't help? What if it makes things even *worse*?" The poor child sounded frantic now. In her desperate efforts to keep her secret, Becky had clearly done more damage than she could possibly have realized.

Not that Susannah held any grudges against her sister. Whatever had shattered Becky so completely had to be beyond horrendous.

With that in mind, Susannah set aside the two bags she'd found, crossed the concrete floor of the storage unit, and took Ellie into her arms.

The girl began to cry, and it was heartbreaking to hear.

"Let's go home," Susannah told her gently, when she'd rocked her niece back and forth in her embrace for a minute or so. "Nico will be waiting for you. And you need some sleep."

"Is everything going to be all right?" Ellie asked, and the question was almost a plea.

Susannah gave her one last squeeze. "Truthfully, I can't promise that, sweetheart, because life is pretty darned unpredictable, but I give you my word that I'll do everything I possibly can to see that things turn out for the best. Fair enough?"

Ellie sniffled, rested her forehead against Susannah's shoulder for a few moments. "Fair enough," she agreed. "I love you, Aunt Susannah."

Susannah's throat thickened so that she could barely croak out a reply. "And I love you, Eleanor Louise Bennet."

Ten minutes later, they were home again.

Ellie gathered a meowing Nico into her arms and retreated

to her room to put on her pajamas. After brushing her teeth in the bathroom, which was under reconstruction and therefore awkward to use, she joined Susannah at the kitchen table.

With a glass of wine close at hand, Susannah was sorting through the notebooks, trying to put them in chronological order, though that seemed like a losing battle, since neither the journals nor the entries were dated. At that point, she was going mostly by the stages of Becky's handwriting development, ranging from large, loopy, childlike letters to a tighter, plainer stream of words.

In all, there were twenty-two makeshift diaries, all filled with Becky's thoughts, experiences, hopes and fears. Partly because she'd used pencils much of the time, rather than pens, large patches of many entries were smeared or even entirely obliterated.

"You're starting now?" Ellie asked, fetching Nico's box of treats from a shelf and shaking a few into her palm as the cat wound himself around her ankles and purred. She dropped the kibble-like pieces to the floor, and Nico began to crunch away on his midnight snack.

Before Susannah could reply, Ellie took a glance at the clock on the stove and continued. "It's super late. You should get some sleep."

"I know," Susannah answered, one hand resting on the notebook she intended to read first. It would be a little like translating ancient hieroglyphs, she thought wearily, feeling more than a little discouraged. Or some recently discovered version of the Rosetta stone. "I promise I won't stay up too much longer."

Ellie looked benignly skeptical. "Okay," she agreed, with scant conviction.

Once both Ellie and Nico had retreated from the kitchen, Susannah fortified her determination with a sip of wine and picked up one of the oldest notebooks.

She gleaned very little from the first one. It contained accounts of incidents at school, descriptions of boys she liked and girls she *didn't*, but nothing that would indicate the kind of trauma Becky must have endured.

The process was profoundly frustrating.

Exhausted but determined, Susannah perused notebook after notebook, setting a stack of them aside, since nothing in them had caught her attention.

At one fifteen in the morning, her vision began to blur.

She swallowed the last of her wine, rinsed out the glass at the sink, and set it in the drainer to dry. She'd purchased a dishwasher for the place, but hadn't installed it yet.

In the bathroom, she cleansed her face, applied moisturizer, and brushed her teeth.

Too tired to bother with pajamas or a nightgown, Susannah removed her bra and khaki shorts and crawled into bed in her T-shirt and panties.

She was asleep in moments, and soon she was dreaming.

Normally, Susannah's dreams were fleeting and meaningless, like black-and-white movie scenes on fast-forward.

That night, perhaps because she was extra tired and had a lot on her mind, they were so vivid, so lucid that she might have been wide-awake, acting out some hectic drama on the stage of her mind.

Suddenly, a much younger Becky appeared before her, bursting out of the nearby woods, running toward her, screaming frantically, "Run, Susannah! Run!"

Susannah ran toward a building she instantly recognized as the lake house their parents leased every summer. Unlike the family home in suburban Chicago, this cottage was small, with a lawn sloping down to the shore, and it was nearly surrounded by thick foliage and a variety of trees.

"*Run!*" the vision-Becky screeched again. "Get inside, Susannah—*now!*"

A jolt of pure terror rocketed through Susannah's mind's-eye self, and she stumbled forward, toward the front door of the cottage, desperate to reach it and the safety within.

The fear ratcheted to such a height that Susannah was suddenly thrust out of the nightmare at high speed, like a stone from a slingshot. In the next moment, however, her trajectory had reversed, and she was falling and falling.

She landed hard in the waking world, with an actual impact, her skin soaked in perspiration, her breathing fast and shallow, her head so light that everything spun around her. She might have had vertigo.

"*What the—?*" Susannah managed to gasp, struggling to sit up. Failing.

She was still trying to restore her equilibrium when Nico zoomed into the room, like a furry streak, hurtling through the air and landing in the middle of her torso with a visceral *thunk.*

"*Meow??*" the cat inquired, as though demanding an explanation.

As her heartbeat began to slow down, Susannah stroked Nico's silken back.

He progressed from her stomach to her chest and began kneading insistently at her T-shirt. "*Meow?*" he repeated.

"Everything's okay, buddy," Susannah managed to assure him, after a few more unstable moments. "It was just a dream."

Just a dream.

But was it? The experience had felt so real, more like a memory than a random night-play of the mind.

A shiver went through Susannah, recalling the desperation, the frantic terror, in Becky's voice and facial expression.

Search though she did, Susannah could find no recollection of such an incident, yet the reality of it dogged her so strongly that she gently moved Nico aside, got out of bed, and put her shorts back on.

Semi-dressed, she headed for the kitchen, but this time, instead of wine, she brewed a pot of strong coffee.

She wouldn't be doing any more sleeping that night, obviously.

She paced while waiting for the coffee to be ready, buoyed by the delicious scent of it, comforted by the oh-so-ordinary sounds of the process.

When Susannah's cup was filled and she'd reseated herself at the table, with the notebooks before her, Nico jumped into her lap. He was in bodyguard mode, apparently.

If it hadn't been the middle of the night, she reflected, still agitated by the mental residue of the nightmare, she would have gone directly to the hospital and demanded to see Becky.

She'd be turned away at such an hour, naturally, and besides, she could neither take Ellie along with her nor leave her behind, alone in the house.

All of which boiled down to the fact that, for now anyway, she was stuck.

She was stroking Nico and brooding between sips of very hot coffee when her phone, which she'd left on the table earlier, made a familiar *ping* sound.

Curious, and frowning a little, but also grateful for the distraction, Susannah pulled the phone closer and squinted at the screen.

A text message.

From Ian McKenzie.

Say what? By then, it was after two in the morning. Why was he sending texts at that hour?

Susannah tapped at the screen with her index finger, and the message popped up.

Hi, Susannah. Ian here. I hope this doesn't wake you up. No sense in both of us losing sleep.

She paused, biting her lower lip and considering her options.

Finally, out of curiosity—and, yes, a touch of excitement— she replied. **No problem. I can't sleep, so I'm sitting in my kitchen, drinking coffee and waiting for the sun to come up. Why are *you* still awake?**

It was then that she remembered that Ian's ex-wife was back in town. The fact shouldn't have mattered to her, since it was none of her business, but matter it did.

Why can't you sleep? Ian responded.

I asked you first, Susannah replied.

A laughing emoji appeared on Ian's side of the screen. **You're right, you did. I can't sleep because of some family stuff— and because, ever since we first met, I've been wanting to ask you out. On a real date, sans kids.**

Susannah felt a faint thrill that eased the aftereffects of the nightmare considerably. **Sounds good,** she answered. **What kind of date did you have in mind?**

Dinner in Flagstaff?

For the briefest fraction of a moment, Susannah wanted to confide in Ian, tell him the particulars of Becky's situation, show him the notebooks, ask for his insights on the nightmare that had made a good night's sleep impossible.

But, no. She barely knew Ian and, besides, her problems weren't his burden to bear.

Dinner in Flagstaff sounds like fun, she tapped in, after a delay, probably coming off as a lot more light-hearted than she actually was. **When?**

Ian: **Next Saturday? I'll be on-duty Tuesday through Friday.**

Next Saturday it is, Susannah wrote back. **Fancy or casual?**

Which one would you prefer? I'm flexible.

A blush warmed Susannah's face, and her heart was beating a little faster. The residue of the nightmare was almost gone. **Casual,** she answered. **I left all my fancy dresses behind in Chicago. But what about the kids? I'm new in town, and I don't know anyone I'd feel comfortable leaving Ellie with.**

Ian: **I know someone you can definitely trust. Her name is Erma Carlson and she's great with kids. She looks after the twins when I'm working, and her husband—you met him when he came to get Tim Boyd's horse after the accident—takes care of the critters.**

Susannah: **Okay. I'd like to meet Erma first, though.**

Not a problem.

How is Tim doing? Susannah remembered to ask. She'd forgotten to call the hospital to get an update on the injured boy's condition, and that made her feel mildly guilty, though she'd had a lot on her plate ever since she'd arrived in Copper Ridge.

He's recovering, Ian wrote. **It's going to be a long haul, since he's pretty banged up, but the prognosis is good. Tim's a tough kid and he'll be back in the saddle in no time.**

Susannah repressed an urge to ask about Ian's ex-wife and why her arrival had stirred up such a fuss in town earlier. It didn't seem likely that a reconciliation was in progress, given that he'd just invited Susannah on a date, but you never know. Maybe Ian McKenzie was a player.

Go back to sleep, he texted, when she didn't respond to his last message right away. **Tomorrow's another day.**

Susannah responded with a smile emoji and a thumbs-up.

Technically, it was already tomorrow.

And there was no telling what it would bring.

Chapter 8

"Are you sure about this?" Ian asked, standing next to Catherine, who was about to sink into the seat of her rental car. "You're really willing to let Vivian and Mabel stay with me for the rest of the summer?" The twins had asked to live with him permanently, but he knew that wasn't feasible, given how much their mother loved them.

Tears shimmered in Catherine's eyes, though she was smiling. "It's obvious that they want to spend more time with you, Ian. So, yes, I'm sure. I want our daughters to truly understand that I won't be cutting you out of their lives just because I have a new husband now—not to mention four stepchildren, all of whom have issues of their own."

Ian didn't miss the reference to *our daughters*, and he was so grateful that his throat thickened and his eyes burned. He glanced away briefly, blinked a few times, met his ex-wife's gaze again. "Thank you, Catherine," he said, his voice husky.

Catherine stood on tiptoe and kissed his stubbled cheek. It was early in the morning, and he hadn't shaved yet. "Thank *you*, Ian, for loving Vivian and Mabel so much. For taking such good care of them, from the very first." She paused, wiped away a tear of her own. "I really wish things had worked out for us," she finished, very softly.

"Me, too," Ian admitted gruffly. "Just remember—I'll always be your friend, never your enemy. And I'm truly glad that you've found someone you can build a life with."

Catherine sniffled, smiled. "Now, it's your turn," she said. "Susannah Holiday sounds like a prospect, from what the girls tell me."

Just then, the twins hurried out of the barn, where they'd been fussing over Ragamuffin and the other horses. As usual, Dub trotted along behind them, tongue lolling.

Mabel and Vivian flung themselves against Catherine's sides and clung to her, heads tilted back, beaming up at her in pure adoration.

"We'll miss you, Mom," Vivian said.

Catherine bent slightly to kiss each of her daughters on top of their golden heads. "And I'll miss you," she replied. "Both of you. FaceTime next weekend?"

"FaceTime next weekend," the little girls chorused.

Ian grinned, though he was still choked up.

He said nothing; this exchange was a mother-and-daughters thing, and he wasn't about to interfere.

Moments later, after hugging each of the twins separately, Catherine said a tearful good-bye and got into the rental car.

And then she was driving away, heading for the road that ran past Ian's ranch, turning in the direction of town.

Vivian and Mabel stood close to Ian as they watched their mother disappear, and he laid his hands on their shoulders. Squeezed gently.

Mabel was crying, and Dub stepped up to lick her face in sympathy.

She laughed then, and shrieked, "Eeeeew!"

"Let's saddle up and ride," Ian said presently, crouching between the children to look directly into their faces. "Sound like a good idea?"

"The best!" Vivian crowed, running her forearm across her eyes.

Twenty minutes later, Sultan, Ian's gelding, and both the twins' ponies were tacked up and ready to go.

Ian helped both girls mount up, then swung up onto Sultan's back.

Dub, refusing to be left behind, made a dash through the outer gate of the corral the moment Ian had leaned over, worked the latch and shoved.

He chuckled, shook his head, readjusted his hat, widening the opening with a motion of one booted foot.

The sun was dazzling that morning, and both girls had hats of their own, bouncing against their little backs as they trotted their ponies through the gap.

At a pointed glance from Ian, they donned their head coverings.

After he'd closed the gate again, he and Sultan led the way toward the nearby foothills, closely followed by the twins and, of course, Dub.

For nearly two hours, Ian and his daughters simply rode, following trails that wound through the hills, pausing beside a bubbling spring to water the horses and stretch their own legs. Walking to the nearby ridge, while Sultan and the ponies grazed, untethered, on rich, green high-country grass, the three of them surveyed the sprawling stretch of land that had been in Ian's family for the better part of a century.

Ian was careful to keep the kids well back from the edge of the jutting boulders that formed the ridge itself, and he was amused to see that Dub was guarding them, too.

It was then that he noticed the blue SUV, far below, turning in at the gate.

"Looks like we have company," he said quietly.

"That's Susannah's car," Vivian announced. "Ellie showed us pictures."

Ian made no comment. He simply pulled his phone free of the clasp on his belt, thumbed the screen, and started a text.

The twins and I are up on the ridge, but we'll be down soon.

Below, Susannah's tiny figure responded with a wave.

The little girl, Ellie, was beside her.

Ian's phone dinged with a response. **Sorry to just show up like this,** Susannah responded, **but I need some advice.**

He replied with a thumbs-up and steered the girls back toward the horses.

Twenty minutes later, when they reached the outside gate of the corral fence again, Susannah was waiting to swing it open for them. Ellie, meanwhile, standing on the lowest rail and gripping the next one up, enjoyed riding the thing backwards.

Susannah's expression, unlike her niece's, was solemn.

She followed Ian into the cool shade of the barn. "I shouldn't have interrupted your ride," she said, looking worried.

Ian made quick work of cooling down the three horses and then putting them up for the night while the twins and Ellie ran around outside, playing some game with the tireless Dub, who was yipping for joy.

"It's not a problem, Susannah," Ian said quietly, tugging off his worn leather gloves and resettling his hat.

Her smile was tentative, delicate. "You really *are* a cowboy," she observed, momentarily distracted, it seemed, from whatever it was she wanted to discuss.

Ian ached to kiss her, then and there, but it wasn't the right time, and he knew it.

"Sans cows," he confirmed, with a slight smile.

With that, Ian took Susannah's elbow in a light grip and steered her out of the barn and toward the house.

They were in the kitchen when she pulled a small, beat-up notebook from the hip pocket of her jeans and waggled it back and forth between a thumb and a forefinger.

"You know about my sister Becky's mental problems, I presume?"

The girls were still outside, with Dub. Ian pulled back a chair at the table and waited for Susannah to sit down. When she had, he nodded and replied, "Yes. Copper Ridge is a small place; everybody knows everybody else's business. And I was on duty when the 911 call came in."

Tears filled Susannah's violet-blue eyes.

Distractedly, Ian wondered if the color was real, or if she was wearing contacts.

When he caught a glance at her profile on his way to the fridge for two bottles of cold water, the question was answered. No contacts.

She was still fiddling with the notebook when he set the water bottles down in the middle of the table and took a seat across from her.

"Talk to me, Susannah," he said, very quietly.

Susannah pushed the notebook in his direction, her hand trembling. "We've always known something really bad happened to Becky, something that traumatized her, but we were never able to find out what it was. My parents took her to counselors, psychiatrists, pastors—none of them could get her to talk."

Ian picked up the notebook, thumbed through it, raised his gaze to Susannah's face. He wanted to take her into his arms, hold her, comfort her.

Again, it wasn't the time.

"And something in here"—he lifted the notebook for emphasis—"explains it?"

Susannah looked broken. Miserable. "Partly," she answered, in a near whisper.

Ian reached across the table and took her hand, held it with gentle firmness. Waited.

Tears slipped down her cheeks.

"Go on," Ian urged, after a few moments, still holding her hand.

"Last night, I had this nightmare," Susannah began, looking everywhere but at him as she spoke. "It sparked a memory—not right away, but eventually, and that memory started unfolding—"

Ian nodded. Remained silent.

"I know what happened," Susannah murmured.

This time, Ian couldn't restrain himself. He stood up, eased Susannah to her feet, and pulled her into his arms.

She hesitated, stiffened slightly, then relaxed into his embrace, resting her forehead against his chest. It was then, odd as it seemed, that Ian first realized he loved this woman.

It didn't matter that he barely knew her; something within her joined with something in him, and he realized then that nothing would ever be the same.

Of course, he knew he would have to think about the attraction he felt toward Susannah later. Right now, she was suffering, and he would have done just about anything to help her.

His lips moved softly against her right temple as he spoke to her.

"I'm listening, Susannah."

She gave a choking sob and wrapped her arms around him. Allowed herself to cling a little.

And it deepened then, that sense of something strong and good connecting them at the deepest possible level.

"Becky's gone through all this because of me!" she whisper-cried, clearly aware that the kids might come inside at any moment. "It was to protect me!"

Ian kissed the top of Susannah's head, then took a light hold on her shoulders and lowered her back into her chair.

Susannah cast an anxious glance toward the open door. Through the screen, the children and Dub were visible, running in circles.

Ian sighed affectionately and took Susannah's hand again. "Tell me," he reiterated, his voice gravelly.

It was sinking in by then that Susannah must trust him a lot, if she was willing to confide her troubles to him like this.

That was when Susannah began to relate her—and Becky's— story.

Ian had seen and heard a lot, as a paramedic, but this tale pinned him to his chair like an arrow shot straight through his heart.

Susannah talked, and he listened.

It was an evil tale, a tale of deception, cruelty and fear, and, listening to it, then scanning the confirming pages in the battered little notebook, Ian wanted to track down the person responsible and wear out his fists on them.

"My God," he muttered, when Susannah had finished.

She was clearly exhausted, shoulders drooping, head down.

Natural as anything, Ian pulled her onto his lap.

"I don't know what to do," she said, her voice muffled by the side of his neck.

"To start with," Ian responded, stroking her back, "we're going to talk to Becky. Maybe she'll open up a little, once she knows we've figured things out. After that, we'll go to the police."

Susannah nodded, but didn't lift her head.

Ian was glad of that, because she would have seen the barely contained fury in his eyes.

"Why did she keep this to herself?" she whispered finally, sounding even more miserable than before.

"Because the jerk threatened you," Ian replied softly. "He was a threat to Becky as well, and then to Ellie. He probably told her he'd kill one or all of the people she loved, if she spoke out."

"But *she married him,*" Susannah agonized. "How could she have done that?"

"Maybe she didn't think she had a choice," Ian answered. Then, he got to his feet, reached for his phone and placed a call to Erma Carlson, asking if she'd mind looking after Vivian, Mabel and Ellie for a few hours. He didn't offer an explanation, but Erma must have guessed, perhaps from his tone, that there was something serious going on.

Erma kindly agreed, telling Ian she was coming straight to his place, and she'd stay as long as she was needed.

Ian thanked her, considering calling the police, and decided to put that off until he and Susannah knew more.

Chapter 9

"Becky," Susannah said firmly, standing in front of her sister's chair in the small room she'd occupied since her admission to the psychiatric ward of Community Hospital. "Look at me."

Becky lifted her face, and her gaze landed on the tattered notebook Susannah was holding out, then bounced up to meet Susannah's.

She said nothing, though she did glance Ian's way, and recognition showed in her otherwise hollow eyes.

Beside Susannah, Ian shifted slightly, but said nothing.

Becky's shoulders slumped, and her chin wobbled. "You know, then," she murmured, in a voice as broken as her mind. "About Roy?"

She was referring, Susannah knew, to Roy Pendleton, Becky's no-good, waste-of-skin ex-husband. And, unfortunately, very possibly Ellie's biological father.

"Yes," Susannah replied simply. She dropped the notebook into Becky's lap, pulled up another chair, and sat down to face her sister. Then, before going on, she took out her phone and set it to a voice-recording app. "I had no idea you knew Roy when we were kids."

In the next moment, shame splashed across Becky's face.

Then she nodded. "He lived in that big house across the fields from the lake cottage Mom and Dad used to lease every summer—with his grandparents."

Susannah sat back in her chair, sighed. This was more than Becky had said in weeks, if not months, and although the words came out ragged, there was an undercurrent of courage flowing beneath them.

Ian's hand came to rest on Susannah's shoulder, and that gave her the strength to press on. "What was he like?"

Becky expelled a breath, a sound of mingled disgust and sorrow. "Roy was a *terrible* person, a bully," she responded, after some time and with obvious difficulty. "But he had all the grown-ups fooled. He was popular in high school and he had all kinds of friends. He used to mow the lawn at the cottage every weekend, in fact—Mom and Dad thought he was great—so we kind of knew him, you and I both. You were young, so maybe you've forgotten."

It was true. She *had* forgotten Roy,

Exhausted, both emotionally and physically, Becky paused then, shaking a little.

Tears wet her cheeks, and her nose was running.

Susannah waited as patiently as she could, though her own nerves were pulled so taut she thought they might snap. Maybe she and her sister could share a room here in the psych ward.

Anxious to hear Becky's version of the story she'd pieced together from entries in the notebook and the memories the nightmare had sparked, she rummaged through her purse, handed Becky a packet of tissues.

Presently, Becky went on. "O-one day," she stammered, "when Mom got a call from a neighbor, just down the road, she sort of panicked and rushed off, telling me to keep an eye on you until she got back."

Susannah vaguely remembered that; an old lady their mother

knew from church had called, evidently in the midst of some crisis.

Becky continued, after another long pause. "We should have stayed in the yard. We weren't supposed to go into the water or the woods without an adult close by—i.e., Mom or Dad—but I was a stupid kid." She shook her head. Waited a few tremulous beats. The energy she was expending must have been of epic proportions. "We were following a path through the trees, and all of a sudden, you ran ahead of me, laughing when I yelled at you to come back."

Susannah's stomach did a flip. She'd recalled this part, after the nightmare, when parts of the story began to unfold in her mind. And she dreaded hearing it verified.

"He was there, in the field—Roy Pendleton, I mean. I guess it was more of a clearing, really, because nothing had been planted there in years, according to Dad. Anyway, he was with two of his friends—" Becky closed her eyes tightly and trembled so hard that Susannah slid to the edge of her chair and pulled her sister into a brief, tight hug.

By then, Ian had retreated to a third chair, now holding Susannah's phone.

"Two of them were wearing these horrible masks—those awful ones with lumps and scars and bloodstains, and—" Becky broke down then, completely, and began to sob, though she managed to choke out, "And Roy was getting ready to pull his on over his head."

Susannah filled in the conversational gap. "And they were burying something—or *someone*," she said. "Right there in the field, alongside some tall bushes."

Becky managed a nod. "Where the blackberries grew. That was where we were headed, initially."

Time was running out; if they didn't finish this terrible exchange soon, a nurse or orderly would enter the room and advise Susannah and Ian to leave, immediately.

"Th-they grabbed you, Susannah—they were laughing like fiends—tossing you back and forth between them. Laughing and laughing." Becky stopped, shook her head again. "They were about to throw you into the hole they'd dug, when I tore off a branch of thistles and hit Roy with it, screaming for them to stop. To leave my sister alone.

"In the confusion—I got Roy good, he was bleeding through his T-shirt—and he came at me. By then, he'd thrown aside his mask and honest to God, I think he meant to kill me. Kill both of us."

"That was when I got away," Susannah supplied numbly. "The other two guys were distracted by your attack on Roy. You screamed at me to run, and I did. I was so afraid." She stopped, met Ian's calm gaze for a moment, found strength in it, then asked, "Why didn't they chase us, Becky?"

Just then, she was realizing how deeply she'd suppressed all memory of that terrible day. Maybe, in her own way, she'd been as traumatized as Becky; she'd simply reacted differently.

"They *did* chase us," Becky said quietly, probably picking up on Ian's grounding energy herself. Drawing from it. "Roy caught me by the hair and yanked my head back. He said if I ever told anybody about that hole by the bushes, he'd kill you and bury you along with the last person who'd crossed him. Then he'd finish Mom and Dad and everybody else I loved."

Susannah closed her eyes.

So there *had* been a body lying in that makeshift grave. Were there others, long-hidden and overgrown by weeds and grass?

"You believed him?" Susannah said. It wasn't actually a question, more of a statement, though it was followed by, "You've kept a secret like that all these years? Mom and Dad would have known what to do, Becky. They would have kept us safe."

"Would they?" Becky countered, looking and sounding completely sane, as though revealing and acknowledging the truth had brought her back from wherever she'd been since her most recent collapse. "You have no idea what Roy Pendleton is capable of, Susannah. No idea at all."

"Fill me in," Susannah said, her voice tightening. She was partly relieved and partly infuriated with Becky for not immediately telling the truth about what happened.

But, then, she hadn't told anyone, either. And, soon enough, she'd repressed the experience entirely.

"For *years* after that incident in the clearing, Roy made a game of putting on that mask and peering at me through windows, always at night, of course. He'd tilt his head back and forth, like the madman he was, and then put a finger to his lips, warning me to keep quiet or else."

"For years," Susannah echoed. "We were only at the lake cottage in the summertime."

"It happened in Chicago, too, Susannah," Becky said.

"And yet you *married* that monster?" All the disbelief Susannah felt was evident in her voice.

Ian caught her eye and raised his brows. "Easy," he mouthed.

Susannah drew a deep breath. Let it out very slowly. "Becky, how could you have actually married him, knowing what you knew?"

"He showed up at the café where I was working at the time, nicely dressed and looking like a preacher. There was actual kindness in his eyes. He ordered coffee and told me he was sorry for scaring us that summer." Becky seemed to be drifting now, gliding back toward some hiding place in her brain. "He said they were burying a dog they'd found dead along the roadside that day, that was all. And he claimed he hadn't been the one to haunt me, on and off for years. Said it was probably one of his friends. He really did seem sorry."

"And then?" Susannah prompted, feeling sick to her stomach.

"And then," Becky said, her words coming out weighted and slow, "one thing led to another, and we got married."

"My God," Susannah exclaimed, though quietly. They had

to get the whole story recorded, find a way to make a case, before some staff member picked up on Becky's distress and sent her and Ian packing. "*Why*, Becky? Why didn't you tell me?"

"You would have disapproved, like Mom and Dad did."

Susannah gave a sigh, exasperated. "Whatever," she said. "Anyway, you've always been pretty, and guys fell for you right and left. Why choose him, of all people?"

Becky met her sister's gaze. "I really thought he'd changed," she said sadly. "Mom and Dad were pissed because I refused to go to college, among other things, so I couldn't bring myself to ask for their help."

Since Becky now seemed about to nod off, or float away into some other dimension or realm, Susannah had to struggle to keep herself from gripping her sister's shoulders and shaking her. Hard.

Fortunately, that wasn't necessary, because suddenly Becky rallied and went on. "He didn't seem to mind that Ellie wasn't his child—I told him about Dave, the guy I dated before him. One thing led to another, and Roy said he liked Arizona, and it was a good place to raise a kid, so we moved here—to Copper Ridge, I mean. I loved it here, especially after Ellie was born. I had mom-friends, and a job, working nights at the Rocking Rocket Saloon, serving drinks, and the tips were better than all right."

Susannah, though profoundly relieved by the revelation that Ellie didn't share Roy Pendleton's despicable genes, felt drained, broken. She remembered the feel of Ian's arms around her, in the kitchen back at the ranch, and found solace in the recollection. In his nearness.

Except for a hello directed at Becky, he hadn't said a single word since they'd stepped into the room almost an hour before, yet the way he listened was almost palpable, a powerful force in its own right.

"But things didn't work out, between you and Roy?" Susannah prompted carefully. Of course she knew they hadn't; knew Becky's insane husband had deserted the family after a few years. But she wanted the full story.

Becky shook her head. "We were okay for a while. Then, he quit his truck-driving job and took to haunting the local bars, including the Rocket, at all hours of the day and night. One evening, when I was off work because Ellie had a fever, he came home in a mood, stinking of booze and acting like a wild man. He accused me of cheating, and bounced me off the walls a few times.

"I was scared for Ellie, and for myself, so I told him to leave or I'd call the cops. And that set him off all over again. I guess it reminded him of what had happened that day in the clearing.

"He left, and I was grateful, but then the harassment started up again. He'd just appear at the living room or bedroom window, always after dark, or in the parking lot at the Rocket when I got off work at two in the morning. He wore those hideous masks, and every time, he reminded me to keep my mouth shut."

Becky looked directly at Susannah, and her voice was surprisingly strong when she spoke again. "Finally, he started sending texts from various burner phones—texts with pictures of *you*, Susannah. In Chicago, out with your friends, in the supermarket, playing with Nico –stuff like that. He was letting me know that he could hurt you anytime he chose. And that's when I finally broke down—too many things were coming at me from too many directions—I was terrified for you, for Ellie and for myself. Ellie was having problems at school, and I lost one job after another."

At last, Ian entered the conversation. "Have you seen Pendleton recently?" he asked. "Or heard from him?"

"No," Becky answered, with another shake of her head and a shudder. She looked small and defeated, a bird with a broken wing, ready to give up. Susannah suspected her sister would have done exactly that, if it hadn't been for Ellie, and, undeniably, for Susannah herself.

Sure enough, Becky stiffened in the next instant. "Where is Ellie right now? Is she safe?"

"Your daughter is fine," Ian assured her. "In the care of a good friend of mine."

Becky's gaze traveled quickly between Ian's face and Susannah's. "You trust this friend?" she asked, of both of them.

It was Ian who replied. "She's looking after my kids, too. Believe me, she won't let anyone hurt them."

Susannah recalled her meeting with Erma Carlson back at the ranch, and silently agreed. Erma was a big woman, muscular and confident; she'd take good care of Ellie, Vivian, Mabel and even Dub.

Just then, a nurse appeared in the doorway.

"Time's up," she said cheerfully. "Ms. Bennet needs to rest."

Ian nodded, but said nothing.

"What happens now?" Becky asked. Since she was looking at Ian, instead of Susannah, he was the one to answer.

"We let the police take it from here," he said, already thumbing the screen of his phone. "And you take hold and start living your life again, for your own sake and for Ellie's."

Becky's face shown with a soft, fragile smile. "I'm going to be strong from now on," she vowed, gazing at Susannah. "Like my sister."

Chapter 10

They parted in the hospital's main lobby, Susannah planning to hide out in the women's restroom for a few minutes, in an effort to recover her equilibrium by breathing deeply and splashing her face with cold water, her customary response to stress.

Ian squeezed her hand and headed outdoors, his phone already pressed to his ear. He was outlining Becky's story for someone at the Copper Ridge Police Department.

When Susannah had calmed her tumbling stomach and churning emotions, she joined him on the hospital's wide concrete steps.

With a gentle glance in her direction and an arm wrapping around her waist, Ian finished the call, pulled her close and, right there in front of God and everybody, the warm sun driving out the chill of all they'd learned, he kissed her.

The kiss was deep, and thorough in a way that made Susannah's insides ache, as though opening to receive and enfold something longed-for but never really expected.

"Everything's going to be all right," Ian said, when he finally drew back.

Susannah's knees immediately buckled, but he caught her. Held her up. "That was some kiss," she murmured, still recovering.

Ian laughed gently, cupped her chin in one hand. "Lady," he ground out, his eyes twinkling with amusement and promise, "you ain't seen nothin' yet."

His words sent waves of heat through Susannah, ones completely unrelated to the high-country climate. She'd long since made a private promise to herself that she'd never have sex with any man until she was married to him, a challenge in the modern-day world, but in those moments, she wondered if she could fulfill that particular pledge.

Ian made her feel things she'd never even imagined feeling before.

And that had been the case, she realized now, since the day they met.

With a rather knowing smile, Ian took Susannah's hand and they descended the steps, then made for the parking lot.

Susannah was blushing the whole way, and once she was seated in the passenger seat of Ian's truck, seat belt fastened, she turned, trying to hide her face from him, embarrassed by her naiveté. But then, because she was strong, as Becky had said, she faced him.

"I have a secret," she confided quietly.

"Interesting," Ian replied, his hands resting on the steering wheel. He'd made no effort to start the engine. "Care to share?"

"That's poetry," Susannah said, with a grin that felt good on her face. Unforced. Natural. "And, yes, I'll share." She gestured for him to draw closer, and he leaned her way, so she could whisper in his ear.

He listened, drew back, contemplated her thoughtfully. "I see," he said. "You realize, I presume, that I can't make the same claim?"

Susannah smiled. "Well, you were married, so—"

"So, when the time comes, I'll be more than happy to show you the ropes. Provided things get that far, anyway."

Susannah was mildly troubled. She loved this man, she'd realized that quite soon after they met, though she had worried she was jumping to romantic conclusions, but the phrase "provided things get that far" had given her pause.

Fearful of saying the wrong thing, making a fool of herself and, worst of all, being rebuffed by the first man she had ever wanted in the world-shifting way she wanted Ian McKenzie, she fell silent.

Ian was quiet, too, until they were on the road back toward Copper Ridge. "Stay for supper?" he asked. "I'm a decent cook."

"Sounds nice," Susannah said. It wasn't the real date he'd promised her, but that was scheduled for the following weekend anyway. She told herself it would be good for Ellie, sharing a meal with her friends Vivian and Mabel.

Ian's eyes were on the road, but he was smiling, and that put solid emotional ground under Susannah's feet. How was it possible that a man's smile, the sound of his voice, his mere *presence*, in fact, could uplift her the way it did?

They hadn't known each other for very long, and yet, from the beginning, Susannah had felt as if she'd known—and loved— this man through multiple lifetimes. He was a stranger who had never *been* a stranger.

And that, she supposed, was why no question, no topic of conversation, seemed out-of-bounds with him.

"Have you ever been to Chicago?" she asked, wanting to verify her take on the matter.

Ian glanced her way. "I went to college in the Windy City," he responded, unexpectedly. "For a couple of years, anyway."

"Did you like it there?"

Ian shrugged. "It was all right. I'm not overly fond of big cities, and I've never liked anyplace as much as I like the ranch." He paused, favored her with a reassuring grin. "My turn to ask—what do you think of Copper Ridge?"

"It's quaint. Friendly. I like it a lot."

"Enough to stay after Becky and Ellie are back on track?"

Susannah hesitated. "Well, I have clients in Chicago. Friends. A house-flipping project I put on hold to come and look after my family. Plus, a nice condo that I own outright."

"I see," Ian responded, his tone noncommittal.

"Just now, Ian, I'm not sure what I want, when it comes to staying or going," she said. *But I definitely want you.*

"I'm thinking we can figure out a plan together," Ian reflected.

"Fair enough," Susannah replied, and that was the end of that particular conversation, at least for a while.

The coming weeks passed as swiftly as if they'd been on fast-forward.

The FBI took on the Roy Pendleton case, since there were interstate elements, including his time in Copper Ridge.

Roy was tracked down quickly and arrested, along with his two high-school cohorts, and charged with first-degree murder, stalking, and a panoply of other lesser crimes, though all of them were felonies.

Further investigation proved that the body in the field-grave near Susannah and Becky's childhood summer home was a teenage runaway named Callie Freeman. Later, to everyone's surprise and horror, other bodies were found in other locations nearby.

With Roy incarcerated, and unlikely to win himself a verdict of "innocent," essentially off the streets and out of the picture for good, Becky began to gain emotional ground with every passing day.

After a month, she was released from the hospital, and in the late summer, funded by Susannah, she and Ellie moved to Chicago, taking up residence in a quiet neighborhood with parks and tree-lined streets and good schools. There, Becky, who planned to study nursing, would continue receiving treatment and Ellie could make a fresh start.

Throughout that busy time, Susannah and Ian spent a lot of time together.

They went on formal dates, shared home-cooked meals, and talked.

They talked and talked, about everything.

They went on long horseback rides and Susannah made lots of new friends, and became involved in community projects, like food drives and animal rescue.

Then, too soon, it was time for Vivian and Mabel to return to Florida for the new school year. Susannah had become very attached to the twins, and she knew she would miss them, but, of course, their departure was harder on Ian—and poor, sweet Dub—than anyone.

Ian flew with the kids to Miami, while Susannah stayed in Copper Ridge, in the almost-finished flip-house, with Dub and Nico, who gave each other a wide berth for the first few hours but then developed a cautious camaraderie.

Knute and Erma Carlson looked after the horses.

When Ian returned, a day later, Susannah met him at the airport in Flagstaff.

His face lit up when he saw her there, waiting.

He dropped his carry-on bag, took her into his arms and, for a moment, buried his face in her hair.

"You okay?" she asked, after a few moments.

Ian straightened, looked into her eyes, and answered, "Yeah," in a low, gruff tone.

Susannah gave him a hard squeeze and changed the subject. "I've been thinking," she said. "You really ought to update the ranch house. I know it holds a lot of good memories, but—"

Ian interrupted by touching her nose and saying, "*I* think

we ought to build a new place. Maybe up on the ridge. As you know, the view from there is amazing."

Susannah stared at him, barely aware of the crowds moving around them, completely focused on the word "we." "But I thought you'd want to live in the old place forever," she finally replied. "Because of your grandparents and everything."

Ian shook his head, picked up his bag in one hand and touched Susannah's slightly heated cheek with the other. "It's time for a few changes," he told her quietly. Then, for what seemed like a very long moment, he looked deep into her eyes, so deep that she felt a tender touch to the soul.

"Such as?" Susannah asked, full of hope.

"Such as, this isn't the most romantic place in the world, and I don't have a ring handy," Ian answered, "but I can't hold back any longer. I've loved you since the first time I saw you, Susannah. Will you marry me?"

All the noise and activity of the airport seemed to fade away; Susannah's heart swelled. "I've loved you just as long, Ian McKenzie," she replied, "and, *yes*, I'll marry you."

"What about Chicago?" Ian asked. They were moving again now, making their way through the flow of departing and arriving travelers, toward the nearest exit.

"I love the place," Susannah admitted. "But I love you more. Maybe we can work out some kind of compromise—a back-and-forth kind of thing, time here, time there. And there are certainly stables where you could board your horses, if you wanted to take them along—we'd keep Dub with us always, of course. Meanwhile, we can build that house you were talking about. I can do most of my web design work remotely, and planning the new place will keep both of us pretty busy."

They were outside by then.

Horns honked.

People shouted greetings and farewells to each other.

"Not a bad idea," Ian conceded, as they headed for the parking area where Susannah had left her SUV. "I'd rather not transport the horses to the big city, though. Let's just hire a ranch hand or two, and spruce up the old house a little so they'd have a place to stay."

Susannah hesitated as they waited to cross the busy road, then went for broke. "You'd really do that, Ian? Leave the ranch for part of the year? Let someone else look after your horses?"

"I'd really do that," Ian confirmed. "I love you, Susannah. And we can come back here anytime we want."

The crossway light, a green hand, shone brightly, and they moved on, entering the parking garage.

They found the SUV, and Ian tossed his bag into the back seat, but instead of opening the passenger door for Susannah—he always drove when they were together—he pressed her against the side of the vehicle and kissed her again.

She nearly fainted from the pleasure of being in such close, primal contact with the man she loved. It was almost better than she imagined actual sex would have been.

Almost.

"I'm going to want babies," Ian informed her, withdrawing only slightly. "You good with that?"

"Very good with that," Susannah assured him.

"Great," Ian answered. "Let's go buy a ring."

Epilogue

One Year Later
Christmas Eve

"This is an amazing house," Becky said. She and Ellie had just arrived from Chicago for the holidays, having flown to Flagstaff, picked up a rental car and driven to Copper Ridge and then to the ranch. Both of them glowed with well-being.

They'd be staying for a full week, and Susannah was thrilled.

"I couldn't *believe* the view," Becky enthused, peering out into the semi-darkness. "The sunsets must be spectacular!"

The Christmas tree was huge, lit up and sparkling in the twilight, and there were piles of beautifully wrapped gifts beneath it. Ellie, now fourteen, was subtly scoping out the loot, much of which was tagged with her name.

"So are the sunrises," replied Susannah. "Just wait until morning; on the other side of the house, you'll see the whole landscape draped in glittering snow."

They were standing before the wide, floor-to-ceiling window overlooking much of the ranch, and Susannah rested one hand on her sizable baby bump, smiled with quiet joy and, yes, a touch of pride. She and Ian had designed the place together, spreading huge sheets of paper over the kitchen table down in the original place and making changes and refinements until they finally agreed the design was as perfect as they could make it. And both of them had carefully overseen the construction phase.

Somewhere along the way, the visits to Chicago had dwindled to the occasional weekend. Copper Ridge, and the ranch, were home to both of them.

Now, the house was finished, with a huge master suite and a sizable home office, among other features, for Susannah, who had continued her web-design business, though she was no longer flipping houses. Between work she enjoyed, a gratifyingly happy marriage and a much-wanted pregnancy, she was plenty busy.

She was thinking about these things when Ian came in from the new and very spacious barn, where he'd been feeding the horses. He'd kept Ragamuffin, and by now, she was part of the family.

Dub, who'd been nestled in for a snooze on a nearby window seat, with Nico close by as usual, jumped down and trotted over to greet him, and Ian crouched to ruffle the dog's ears. The affection between the two often touched Susannah so deeply that tears burned in her eyes.

Meanwhile, Becky turned to grin at her brother-in-law and joked, "I guess you two have literally come up in the world."

Ian chuckled, his eyes fond. "Hey, Becky. Ellie." He greeted the welcome guests, crossing the large living room, with its rafters and skylights and gleaming hardwood floor, to hug both of them, then proceeding to kiss Susannah's cheek and cover her hand, where it rested on her swollen middle, with his own.

Ellie was growing up to be an exceptionally pretty young woman and, like her mother, she was thriving in their new life in Chicago. She was getting good grades, taking riding and dance lessons, and studying Spanish.

Best of all, she had plenty of friends. Good ones.

Becky was doing well in both nursing school and therapy, and she was dating a very nice guy named Charles King.

Susannah and Ian had met Charles during one of their stays in Chicago, and they'd liked him. He was an RN and he and Becky had met at one of many training sessions at a local hospital, felt an instant connection and, after spending a lot of time together outside the school/work environment, they'd fallen in love.

Susannah understood instant connections. It had been that way for her, and for Ian, too. The moment she'd met her now-husband, she'd been struck by the intangible substance of him, the innate strength and goodness of a man who made caring for the injured and sick his life's work.

And when Ian wasn't serving as a paramedic, he was helping neglected horses recover from trauma. He was a dedicated father to his two stepdaughters, Vivian and Mabel, loving them with all his heart, and eagerly looked forward to their summer visit.

Susannah smiled to herself. She'd gotten lucky, she knew, and Ian insisted that *he* was the lucky one. It was a thing they pretend-argued about.

Ellie beamed at him. "Can I ride Ragamuffin, Uncle Ian?" she asked. "I've been learning a lot, taking lessons and practicing like crazy."

Ian grinned, gave his niece a one-armed hug. "Yes," he said. "You can ride Ragamuffin. She's a lot stronger than she was before." He paused. "Actually, your Aunt Susannah and I have been talking about it, and we've decided she ought to be your horse. You can ride her whenever you visit. Good idea?"

Ellie let out a shriek of glee and hugged him.

She visited Ian and Susannah often, mostly during school

breaks, and she was especially fond of Ragamuffin, maybe because she and the little mare had much in common; both of them had been through a lot of pain and trouble and come out as winners.

"Really?" Ellie cried, evidently still grappling with the surprise. "I get to have *my very own horse?*"

"That's the plan," Ian confirmed, turning to Becky. "Is that okay with you?"

Becky looked almost as pleased as her daughter. "Of course it is!" she replied happily. Tears glimmered in her eyes as she looked from Ian to Susannah. "You two have been so good to us—"

She was referring, Susannah supposed, to the emotional and financial support they'd given her and Ellie, so they could begin living as they deserved to, and as far as Susannah was concerned, the investment was entirely worthwhile.

"Thank you." With a half sob, Becky moved to hug her sister, bumped into her prominent stomach, and laughed as the two of them bounced away.

Susannah laughed, too. And cried.

Hours later, when they'd shared a lively FaceTime call with Vivian and Mabel, far off in Miami, enjoyed a delicious supper together, watched a holiday movie on TV and watched as Ellie hung a giant felt Christmas stocking, made by Susannah, it was time for bed.

They'd be up early, as they were every day, with chores to be done, chores they shared, although Ian did all the heavy work.

"Susannah?" Ian said, as his wife snuggled close to him.

Beyond the big windows, fat flakes of snow danced and swirled.

She tilted her head just far enough to kiss the underside of his chin. "What?"

"Merry Christmas," he answered. "And a happy Forever."

She smiled in the darkness. "Merry Christmas, darling. And

as long as I can be with you—hopefully forever—I'll love you just as much as I do now. Incredibly. Fathomlessly."

He laughed quietly. "Next year, we'll be a family of three," he said. "What shall we name our firstborn son, Mrs. McKenzie?"

"Well, Mr. McKenzie, I was planning to surprise you in the morning, but I guess I'll tell you now."

Ian rose up and rested his head in one hand, studying her face as best he could, with all the lights out. "*What?*"

Susannah giggled, traced his lips with the tip of one index finger. "As you know, I saw my OB guy a few days ago. Turns out, the earlier sonograms were inaccurate." She paused, letting the moment stretch just a little too far.

"Susannah." Ian's tone wasn't exactly terse, but it was clear he was getting frustrated.

She relented. "We're having twins, Ian. Both boys."

Ian gave a shout of joy that probably awakened both Becky and Ellie, who were on the other side of the house, sharing the largest guest room.

Then he drew her to him, firmly but very gently, and kissed her in the same thorough way he always did.

"Twins!" he rasped, as if he couldn't believe it.

"Twins," she confirmed, with a happy sniffle.

"Joshua," he suggested presently, in a very solemn tone.

"I kind of thought we agreed on that already," Susannah murmured. "We need a *second* name. How about 'Ian'?"

"No," Ian protested immediately. "People would call him Junior, and both names start with 'J'. I don't want our sons to feel like extensions of each other, twins or not."

"I guess we'll just have to keep thinking." Susannah sighed.

Ian kissed her again.

And both of them forgot about everything and everyone except each other.

Cowboy, Take Me Away

MAISEY YATES

Chapter 1

Birdie Lennox was no stranger to a bad time. In fact it wouldn't be out of line to say that she was downright cozy with hardship.

But Birdie had also decided something crucial at a very early age. Once she had realized that life had filled her welcome basket full of lemons, she had also decided that she was going to throw those lemons right back.

Lemonade was for optimists. Chucking that citrus right back at fate was for fighters.

Birdie had always been a fighter.

And what she really wanted at this point, more than anything, was to get the hell out of Dodge. She had a plan on how to do that.

She had given up trying to get any help from her dad years ago—he was a terrible human being, so there was no point. She also didn't have any friends she could count on in this boring, godforsaken wasteland in the central part of the state of Oregon.

She was tired of listening to the empty words of ridiculous men—who were always happy to promise the world before a woman shared their bed, but delivered crumbs after.

She was self-reliant, but she also knew how to make the best of a bad situation, and make it work for her.

Sometimes self-reliance only got you so far. But right now, she had no one else to help her get off somewhere else. Anywhere else.

And she'd hit on the perfect way to escape—a massive cattle drive out in Texas that paid dream money. The only issue was it was a bring-your-own-horse situation. She did not have a horse.

There was one other person leaving this area and going to the cattle drive—that was where she had found out about it in the first place. And she wasn't blind to the fact that Jamison Holiday was probably expecting payment in the form of sex for the ride.

She would deal with that later. Before she even needed to use his truck and trailer, she had to get a hold of a horse.

And she knew exactly where to get one.

The Lennox family ranch—such as it was—abutted Parsons land.

Gunnar Parsons was, and always had been, a giant hunk of granite. Immovable, unbreakable, implacable. And entirely unfriendly to her.

Their families had a lot of years of bad blood between them. Mostly because the Parsons clan was always accusing the Lennox family of rustling cattle from their property, stealing ranching equipment, animals, and basically anything that wasn't nailed down.

And the Lennox family had a bad habit of doing all those things they were accused of. Made the rift a little bit hard to heal.

It wasn't that Birdie thought stealing was a moral neutral. She didn't. It was just that she couldn't afford to care.

Morality was expensive. And in this economy? She would rather have a horse.

She might not see eye to eye with her old man, but she could respect some of his methods of getting by.

And he had taught her well. Which was how she found herself scrabbling onto Parsons land in the middle of the night with an eye to nabbing one of Gunnar's chestnut mares. The thing was, the guy had a whole slew of horses. He couldn't ride them all at once. And the one Birdie was eyeing wasn't one she'd ever seen the taciturn cowboy ride. Not even once.

You couldn't leave a horse unused. It would go to seed. Go fallow, even. A fate worse than death. Birdie was just moving the animal so that it could have a better quality of life. On the range. Doing actual work.

And Birdie felt her motivation put her several notches above her own father, who stole things to get around work, not to gain admittance to a job.

Birdie took her boots off, and left them standing upright at the edge of the fence. She climbed over the top of it and landed silently on the other side. It was about a hundred paces to the stable from this point. She'd gotten a visual on all of the points where security lights might turn on. She also knew that Gunnar went to bed at like nine o'clock every night, because he was a rancher and he did get up with the sunrise. The dude was as predictable as he was rigid.

She'd lived next door to him all her childhood, so she was familiar.

He was a couple of years older than she, but he wouldn't have been her friend even if they'd been the same age. They were like oil and water. Peanut butter and motor oil. Not a good match. Not even the same kind of thing.

But then, Gunnar didn't know about struggle. Or the kinds of things that you would be willing to do to get out of a fix.

His family always had money. His dad had always worked hard, worked the land and done it well.

Birdie's dad was a bum from way back.

A man who loved whiskey more than he loved his wife and daughter. And then there was her mom, who had loved her freedom more than she had loved her husband or her daughter. Not that Birdie could totally blame her. Living with her dad sucked. Of course, Birdie hadn't signed on for it. She had just been born into it.

Welcome. Basket. Of. Lemons.

Well, she was about to throw those things right back.

She could feel the dirt sticking to the bottom of her socks, and she grimaced slightly. But it didn't deter her. She made a beeline through the part of the pasture where she knew she wouldn't be picked up by any light sensors and managed to press herself up against the side of the barn.

The horses would be in the stable for the night, and she was going to have to hunt around until she found the one she wanted. She had been watching her. Observing her temperament while the animals grazed out in the field. Birdie had a great sense for horses. She always had. Whenever she had honest jobs, they tended to be around horses. But the problem was, it was hard for her to find those jobs, and harder still for her to keep them. It was difficult for her to do anything locally because of her dad's reputation.

And her own. If she were honest.

Whatever. She wasn't going to overthink this. Keeping her back pressed against the wall, she sidled to the back door and took her lock-picking kit out of her pocket. With deft ease, she opened the door like a can of sardines and slipped right inside. She let out a sigh of relief. And kind of wished that she had bothered to carry her boots with her, because all the gunk sticking to the bottom of her socks was starting to really gross her out. And now there were bits of hay stuck there along with dirt.

She pressed the tips of her teeth together, holding her mouth in a grimace as she moved quickly through the stables. She didn't flick the lights on; instead she used the flashlight on her phone to get a visual on the different horses.

There she was.

The mare was at the end of the long row of stalls, with a nameplate on the door that said: Alfalfa Sprout.

"God Almighty," she whispered. "What a terrible name. If you were mine, I would've given you a much more romantic name than that. I think names matter," she said sagely. "I'm Birdie because I was always meant to fly away. And you should be Pegasus. Because you're mythical, and you're going to grow wings and fly with me."

She moved away from the stall, and looked around until she found the tack room, which was also locked. She jimmied that lock too, then rustled up a halter. She crept into the stall, and put her hand on Pegasus's forehead. She let the horse sniff her other hand. And once she was certain that she and the animal had an accord, she led the mare out of the stall and over to the tack room. She felt vaguely nervous about the end part of this scheme, which would include riding out of here without being heard.

And snagging her boots.

She took a hoof pick and a few other items that she could easily fit into her pockets, then grabbed a bridle, a horse blanket and a saddle. She moved quickly, thankful for the years of experience she had, and kept hold of the halter and lead rope, because she might need them later, and she didn't have any money right now to buy a damn thing.

She led the mare out of the barn as quietly as possible, and then, holding her breath, she slung herself up into the saddle. She had led the animal right into another dead zone where they wouldn't set off any lights.

"Are you ready, Pegasus? Because we've got to fly now."

She urged the horse into a fast trot and rode her up and over the fence, a rush of adrenaline spiking in her veins. Then she paused, leapt off and pulled her boots on, grimacing at the crunchy feeling of dirty socks inside her boots. She mounted again and took off down the gravel driveway at a rapid pace.

And suddenly, she heard the sound of a roaring engine and saw bright headlights.

"Oh no," she moaned.

The truck's engine revved, but it didn't move. And the road was so closed in by foliage on either side that Birdie couldn't just go around. She debated ditching the horse, but if she did that, she was never getting out of here. She would never, ever get out of here. She would be stuck. Sisyphus pushing a boulder up the hill, only to have to do it again. Never ending. Never, ever.

She was close to despairing, which was something she never did.

Despair was as expensive as morality, and she didn't have that kind of wealth.

When the truck door opened, her chest seized up tight.

"Well, well. If it isn't Birdie Lennox. Stealing from my land."

She bristled, his voice automatically raising her hackles. "Well, well. If it isn't Gunnar Parsons, out of bed past ten p.m. on a weeknight."

"See, the thing is," Gunnar said, closing the truck door behind him, gravel crunching under his boots as he began to walk toward her, "only one of those things is a surprise."

She blinked. She wasn't exactly sure what he was getting at. Whether he was agreeing that he was totally lame, or calling her a two-bit thief.

Well, two of those things were true. So, she could make a reasonable guess.

She couldn't see his face. It was concealed by the darkness. He was a big, hulking silhouette with the truck lights behind him. Cowboy hat even when there was no reason for him to have it on, broad shoulders, stupidly tall. Truly, there was no reason for a person to be that tall. Stepladders had been invented, so there wasn't an evolutionary purpose to it.

She had a feeling, though, even though she couldn't see his expression, that he was mad.

And Birdie decided right then and there that she was going to do what she did best. Double down. A lesson she had learned early was that people expected a certain thing from a person caught in an outrageous lie. And often, when you defied that expectation, they didn't really know what to do. Often, they started to believe the lie as long as you made it very clear that you believed it all the way to your bones.

Denial was more than a river in Egypt. It was also one of Birdie's very good friends.

"This is actually my horse," she said. "We were just going for a late-night ride."

"The trouble is, that's my horse. I know which horse it is too. Alfalfa Sprout. You set an alarm off inside my stable. And I watched you pilfer her, from my phone."

"That's very weird, because it is not your horse. It's my horse named Pegasus, and Alfalfa Sprout is a stupid name."

"Birdie," he said, his voice as uncompromising as the rest of him. "I saw you. You're caught on camera taking the horse."

"I don't recall such a thing happening."

"I don't care if you recall it or not. I have the video saved on my phone, and I am going to call the police. Which is something my father never did do, because he felt he couldn't prove that your father was stealing."

"News flash: I'm not my father. So even if my father was stealing from you, and he probably was—he's a very unsavory character—it has nothing to do with me. I am as pure as the driven snow. I would never. I was actually out riding because I've been really busy with my volunteer work at the Methodist Church."

"It's not volunteering to sneak into the food pantry and take stuff for yourself."

She had to hold back a snarl. "I haven't done that since I was twelve. I've had a character arc."

"Yeah. You've gone from stealing gummy bears to stealing whole horses. Not really the kind of arc most people go on."

"That just proves they aren't ambitious. Though, I maintain my innocence."

"I don't really care what you maintain. I'm going to call the police."

She felt an icy chill down her spine. It wasn't that she'd never had brushes with the law before. But not since she was a kid. The stakes had been lower back then. A little slap on the wrist, nothing that would linger on her record to the end of time.

But this? She couldn't have a record of her stealing livestock— she really would never get a job working at a ranch again.

"Don't do that," she said.

"Why the hell shouldn't I? You're trespassing. You stole my horse."

"Technically, I've never left the property." She should've known that with Gunnar, doubling down wouldn't work. Because as stubborn as she was, he was more so.

"Doesn't matter. Your intentions are clear."

"Please," she said, hating the fact that there was a note of pleading in her voice. "Just take her back. I have a job. But if I don't have a horse I can't do the job."

"Here's the problem with you, Birdie—you're full of crap. Just like your old man. You always have been. You might have a job. Or you might have intended to load my horse into a shipping container and sell her for meat."

Birdie was legitimately offended by that. "I would never, and have never hurt an animal in my life. I would take better care of this horse than you do. You have so many of them, and I don't even have one."

"Well, I hate to break it to you, but there's no horse distribution system out there making sure there's horse equity."

"Maybe there should be. Office of equine equity."

"I'm not bantering with you in the middle of the night in the middle of my driveway."

"Well, I'm not going to jail. So we are at an impasse."

"Whether or not you go to jail is up to the police officers, not to me."

Feeling defeated, she dismounted. And winced again because she could feel the hay on her socks. "You listen to me. I wanted this horse to make my life better, and I will be damned if I'm going to let you ruin it, Gunnar Parsons. You were born with a silver spur in your ass. And I've never had a damn thing. Not a damn thing that I didn't work for—"

"Is that what you call stealing these days?"

"You inherited all of this. You don't know what it is to struggle. What it is to suffer. How dare you stand there like you're the one up on a high horse."

"You need a job, Birdie?"

She blinked. She was utterly flabbergasted by his question. "Yes. That's what I've been saying. And actually I have one, but I need the horse—"

"I'll tell you what. You can work it off, and I won't call the cops. Your debt, your dad's debt. And I'll save some wages for you in an account. You'll get some money too, once I'm satisfied that there's been restitution made for the years that the Lennox family siphoned cash off of my family."

"I'm sorry, are you suggesting that I work to pay off my father's sins?"

"They're sins that you're participating in. My ranch is not a food pantry. It's not here for you to take things just because you feel like you're in need. It never has been. I don't respect a con. And I sure as hell don't respect a thief. Honest work, that's the only thing I recognize, so if you think you can do that, if you think you can put in an honest day's work here for two months, I'll send you off with a clean slate and a horse."

"I don't have anywhere to stay."

"You can stay in the bunkhouse."

A job with a room? What he was offering her wasn't a bad deal. And if it wasn't bad, it meant it was too good to be true, and that did feel like a conundrum.

She stood there dumbfounded. "But I'll miss the cattle drive."

"I don't give a crap about the cattle drive. You need work— I've got work."

"I want to get out of here. I need to get out of this town."

"Great. I can help you do that. Honestly."

"Why?"

"That isn't any of your business. So what do you think, Birdie Lennox? Do we have a deal, or do I call the cops?"

Begrudgingly, and with gunk in her boots, Birdie took a step forward. And stuck her hand out. "We have a deal."

He shook her hand, and she was surprised by how rough it was. How hot. She had never touched Gunnar Parsons in her life. And why the hell would she?

One thing she knew for certain was that he wasn't offering charity. There was a catch. She was going to find it. And when the moment was right, she was going to throw a lemon right at him.

But for now, she wasn't going to get arrested.

That would do.

Chapter 2

"If you decide to run, I'm only going to call the police."

Gunnar felt overburdened and bone weary. But that was nothing new. And now he had gone and saddled himself with the most irritating urchin he had ever known.

Birdie Lennox had been sneaking around his property for the past three weeks. He knew that she didn't think he'd seen her, but he had. On multiple occasions, skulking around the stables and a few of the different pastures. He knew her family well enough to know that she was up to no good. Hell, no good ever came from a Lennox being on Parsons land. But unlike his father, he had the ranch set up with technology so if somebody tried to rustle one of his animals, he would have proof.

As he did now.

The alarm had gone off while he'd been down at the Cowboy Bar, looking to pick up a date for the evening.

He did that rarely, very rarely, and the fact that Birdie had cockblocked him on top of everything else just made him mad. She was right—it was unusual for him to be up past ten p.m., and if he was, it was with a goal in mind. But instead, he'd had to come back here and deal with an attempted theft.

His father had hated the Lennox family for as long as Gunnar could remember. He had given multiple soliloquies about the dangers of that dissolute family, and their lack of morals. The Parsons family was the salt of the earth. His father had said that often too.

They worked hard; they did the right thing. Always right. And rigid as hell.

Gunnar had often wondered if there was some middle ground there. Between what his father viewed as the right thing and the way the world actually worked. But as long as Jan Parsons was alive, there was no broaching that subject. There was no room for shades of gray. The world was black, or it was white. For the most part, Gunnar agreed.

But that small percentage of the time he didn't . . .

His father would have called the police on Birdie.

He would have said that she deserved it. He would've said that there were no circumstances under which a crime like this could be forgiven or overlooked. The thing was, Gunnar couldn't help but feel sorry for her. She was wretched. And definitely a product of her upbringing. Hell, in much the same way that Gunnar was.

He didn't have it in him to forgive something like this wholly and completely. There would have to be consequences. But the girl needed a job.

"Do you have a vehicle here?"

She shook her head. "No. I was going to ride the horse home."

"Right. Well. Let's head on back up to the house. We can put Alfalfa Sprout back in her stable."

"Pegasus."

"You don't get to name my horse."

"Listen, Gunnar, there is right and there is wrong. Alfalfa Sprout is wrong."

"I'm not going to stand here and take lectures on right and wrong from you."

"You never were one for taking lectures. Only giving them."

"Oh yeah?"

"Oh yeah. In fact, I remember the time that you came and gave all of us a dressing-down out at the swimming hole because we were on your family's land."

"You little termites were trespassing."

He could remember happening upon Birdie and her friends swimming there when they were probably about thirteen and Gunnar was fifteen. He'd run them right off after yelling about property lines.

Against his will, he and Birdie had a history.

You could just send her on her way. You could pretend that this never happened. Because your dad is dead, and he'll never know.

But everything in him rose up against that. He couldn't do that. He couldn't just let her off the hook when . . .

What she was doing was just wrong.

And he couldn't stand for it.

Besides, she had cut a hole in his fence, and she needed to fix it. Also, he was working on expanding the ranch, and he could really use an extra pair of hands. He was missing his dad a lot. Every time he looked at the ranch finances and realized they were dwindling. Because his dad had done things the way he had always done them and had never wanted to change. No, he thought he knew better. Jan Parsons was always convinced that he knew best, and no one else could ever tell him a thing.

Well, that had left him with a ranch that was less and less profitable every year. Which was why Gunnar was expanding. It was why he was getting a bison herd, trying to enter the specialty marketplace so that he could actually be competitive.

And yeah, Birdie was a woman, so it wasn't like she could lift anything heavier than he could, but he knew that she was capable, mean and stubborn as they came. All things that would come in handy while building fences and clearing out brush.

The way he saw it, he could have his pound of flesh, make progress on his project, and finally get repayment from a Lennox. If he never did anything more, this might be enough to make his father proud of him. Even from beyond the grave. But then again, maybe not. Maybe it was impossible to make Jan Parsons proud.

"You ride on ahead of me, and I'll drive behind you."

He could see Birdie's facial expressions, bathed in the headlights as she was. "How do I know you won't run me over?"

He took a step toward her. "Because I would never hurt an animal. Just like you. Wretched thieving villains, on the other hand . . ."

"Great. I'll make sure I keep the horse close by."

"Do that."

She rode slowly, and he knew she was doing it to bother him. To string out this interaction.

He watched the set of her bony shoulders as she rode, and even though he was looking at the back of her head, illuminated by his headlights, and all he could see was her shiny copper ponytail, he was absolutely certain that she was smirking.

Because Birdie was always smirking.

She always had that look about her, as if she knew that she was going to get the best of you. He hated that.

In fact, he had always hated her. Because when they were kids, he had never known what the hell she was going to do next. She didn't follow a logical moral code. And he required that. You did things because they were right, you didn't do them because they were wrong. The end.

Birdie was going to do whatever the hell she pleased.

Sometimes he hadn't been sure whether he hated her or envied her. He knew better now. She was just annoying. There was nothing to envy.

Finally, after making the ride last far longer than was necessary, they arrived back at the barn. He got out of the truck after killing the engine and went to stand by the horse. He looked up at Birdie, who was indeed smirking.

"Well, here we are. I guess you should show me to my room."

"There's time yet. But you need to put away the horse you got out. I'll supervise."

Her smirk twisted into a snarl. But she got off the mare and led her into the barn. She was cooing and talking to it, and using the name Pegasus repeatedly to annoy him. He decided not to take the bait. Something he hadn't been capable of when they were younger.

She took her sweet-ass time, but finally the horse was put away.

"Have you got a change of clothes or anything?"

She shook her head. "No. And my socks are full of hay."

He looked down and stared at the pair of beat-up brown boots she was wearing. "Your socks?"

Then he looked back up at her, at her glittering green eyes, which shimmered like mean little beetles in the light of the barn. "Wouldn't you like to know."

"Well, I'm not taking you back to your place tonight."

"I don't have a place," she said. "Actually, I've been sleeping in the barn over at my dad's. But he doesn't know that."

"You have a go bag?"

"Every shady character worth her salt has a go bag, Gunnar. But you wouldn't know anything about that. You've never thought you might have to run."

More than that, he'd always known he never would. This ranch was his legacy, and there had never been any question of whose responsibility it was to take up that legacy. When his mother and sister had died in a car accident back when Gunnar was five, it had left him and his father alone. The ranch was theirs to uphold. Along with the code of the West.

That was all there was. It was all there had ever been.

"No." He did feel a small surge of pity for her. He didn't want to feel sorry for her. She was pathetic because of her own choices. If she didn't want to be threatened with the consequences of her own actions, then she shouldn't have stolen a horse out of his barn.

Anyway, as consequences went, his were pretty reasonable, if he said so himself.

"Then let me just show you to your quarters. I'll bring you a pair of socks."

"I can just sleep barefoot," she said.

He didn't know why, but that admission felt intimate, and he had never in his life wanted to be anything like intimate with Birdie. No, usually he just wanted to be distant from her, because every *single* time he had to deal with her, she was being a pain in the ass. This time was no different.

Though, maybe because he had gone out with the intent of hooking up tonight, he couldn't help but notice that she really was a very beautiful woman. It was a shame that looks so neat and fine were wasted on such a little weasel. But she had beautiful coppery hair, freckles scattered across her upturned nose, and the kind of full, pretty mouth that would tempt a lesser man to sin.

Too bad Gunnar wasn't interested in sinning.

"Suit yourself," he said. "Come on."

He turned around and walked toward the other end of the stable, to a door that led to the second floor. He unlocked it, opened it. "By the way, the trashed locks will come out of your wages too."

"How do you know that I trashed the locks?"

"Somehow, I just do."

He started to walk up the stairs, and he did not hear Birdie following behind him. He paused and turned. "Are you going to kill me?" she asked.

"No. I'm almost damn near flattered that you think I might."
Because everyone knew that Gunnar Parsons had never set foot
out of line in his life.

"You're flattered that I think you might be a murderer?"

"I don't know if *flattered* is the right word, actually. But it's
definitely something no one has ever asked me before."

"You must live a quiet little life, Gunnar."

Right. A quiet little life. Working the land sunup to sundown
till his sweat soaked into the ground, doing his damnedest to
honor not only his father's memory but his mother's. His sister's memory.

He was the last of his family.

He had never struggled the way Birdie did, but he wasn't a
stranger to how brutal life was. He didn't know if a man could
call his existence *quiet*.

He opened up the door at the top of the stairs and revealed a
neat bedroom that hadn't had anyone living in it for a while. It
had alternatively been used by employees, tenants, and for a
while, him.

There was a desk up against the far wall, beneath the picture
window, a small bed with a metal frame pressed against the wall
next to it. Birdie didn't seem all that impressed.

"You got an issue?"

"Just wondering how the accommodations compare to the
ones down at the county jail."

"We could do a little compare and contrast if you want, but
I thought you wanted to avoid the police."

She offered him a toothy smile, which felt somehow threatening. Too bad for her he didn't find her scary. Just . . .

Birdie.

"Why don't you get in bed."

Her eyes went round, and her brows shot midway up her
forehead. "Oh. It's like that, is it?"

Her cheeks actually went slightly red before her brows lowered again, and he could see that she was considering something.

And right then, he understood. Right then, his gut started to churn. "That is not what I meant," he said.

"Really? Because usually when a man asks me to get into bed . . ."

"Sleep. It's late, and we have to get up early to work."

"You sure?"

For a moment, he felt heat lick through his veins. For a moment, he could only stare at her. But just a moment, because then he came back to himself. Who he was.

"Yes. I'm sure. You're going to have to work off your debt on your feet."

The corner of her lips twitched. "Kinky."

He ground his teeth together. "Go to sleep, Birdie. If you're gone in the morning, I'm sending the cops after you."

"You're literally letting me sleep in the stable? You trust that I won't take off with your horse again?"

"I don't trust you. But I have alarms. And crucially, video, which you already know. You could try. But you won't get very far."

She seemed not to have much to say to that. He turned and left her standing there, and he didn't give her a backward glance. He walked down the stairs and out of the barn, toward the ranch house.

It was a beautiful house. A house that had always been meant for a family, but had ultimately ended up just containing him and his father.

There were so many rooms that he never went in. Vacant bedrooms, a dining room. He just ate in front of the TV. By himself.

When he went inside, he reflexively pulled a bottle of whiskey out of the cabinet.

He marveled at the way his movements mimicked his father's. Jan hadn't been an angry drunk or anything like that. His drinking hadn't caused the problems on the ranch—they were a result of a shifting economy and changing times. But there was never a night his old man hadn't used whiskey to help send him off to sleep.

He was just like his dad. Never anything that caused him to behave poorly. Never anything that caused him to treat people badly.

He never shirked his duties; he never forsook his morals.

But there was a quiet sadness in him that he couldn't seem to talk about. As if grief was a moral failing of some kind, and a man couldn't shed a tear without betraying weakness.

He could drink. He could sit alone in silence.

Push his feelings down.

Gunnar was totally aware of that. Even as he poured himself that drink. As he sat down in silence in the living room, in the leather chair his father used to sit in. What the hell had he done?

He had a cuckoo in the nest.

And no amount of drinking was going to make her go away. He'd set all this up, and now he had to deal with it.

He was not looking forward to tomorrow.

Chapter 3

Birdie woke up with the sunrise, which was unusual for her. Unless she had something to do. But as soon as her eyes snapped open, she remembered. And she found herself tumbling out of bed. Which made the bottom of her foot brush against the back of her knee, and she yelped and started to brush at the hay still on the bottom of her socks.

How had she fallen asleep with these on?

She took them off, then ripped the covers back and brushed all the grit out of the bedding. She hated that. She hated it so much. It was so gross.

She could live rough, honestly. She had done it when necessary, but she liked all of her things to be clean. And definitely not texturally problematic.

She wished she had a change of clothes. She shook her socks out ruthlessly, then put them back on and decided to get dressed and go in search of Gunnar.

Alternatively, she could flee.

Yes. She could do that. She could run away and hope that he didn't call the police on her. She could bank on the fact that he probably wouldn't want to bother. As long as she didn't steal his horse. But she would be stuck without a job. Because she still wouldn't have a horse, so she couldn't work the cattle drive.

She decided she was going to the house. Going to . . . follow this through? If he actually paid her . . . If she ended up with a horse. Of course, once she finished working for Gunnar, she wasn't going to have anywhere to stay. Nowhere to keep the horse.

You'll find other work. You'll find a place to go. You always do.

That was true. She had a way of taking tribulations and turning them into triumphs, and she would do it again.

So she got dressed and headed down to his house, hoping there would be food and coffee, but suspecting it was a vain hope. No matter. She was very good at ignoring being hungry. She had gotten used to it.

She could not get used to hay in her socks, though.

Maybe he would let her borrow a pair. She needed to wash hers. And she needed to get all her supplies.

She stomped up the front steps, then debated between ringing the doorbell and knocking. Ringing the doorbell seemed very noisy. She was trying to decide how intrusive to be when the door jerked open.

"How long are you going to loiter out here?"

She blinked and looked up. He was shirtless. His chest was broad and muscular, with a smattering of golden hair over his pectoral muscles and down his washboard abs. Well. He was hot. Not that she didn't know that. He was handsome, in a very perfectly formed symmetrical sort of way. If you liked disapproving, icy blue eyes that looked like they could cause an avalanche, square jaws and things like that.

Just if you happened to.

What she hadn't realized was that he was hot. Like, hot hot. Like, burn your good intentions to the ground hot.

She had never actually met a man who was that hot.

She only met men who were conveniently hot. Like, secure a room for a couple of weeks and a few meals hot. It wasn't the same.

One was a nice companion piece to getting what you needed. The other was potentially destructive. Very little good could come of it.

At least, in her opinion.

So she decided to ignore his hotness. Difficult to do, because he was so tall, the center of his chest was actually right in her line of sight.

"I'm not loitering. I was trying to decide whether to knock or ring the doorbell. I was trying to not be rude, actually. Because I care about such things."

"I'm sure you do. Come on in."

She could smell bacon, and coffee.

She blinked, as if she was fighting pressure against the back of her eyes, but she couldn't say why. "Can I borrow some socks?"

"What?" He looked at her as though she had grown a second head.

"Socks. Mine are dirty."

"Why don't we go grab your bag before we start work? But sure. I'll go get a pair of socks—they're going to be huge on you, though."

"That's okay."

He returned a moment later with socks in a bundle, and she took her boots off enthusiastically, and changed her socks. Then she went back out onto the front porch and made sure that her boots didn't have any remaining hay inside.

When she came back in, she didn't see him. She walked

through the entryway and into the kitchen, where he was standing, loading up a plate. "Here," he said, shoving it at her. She clamped her fingers around the edge, like claws. "Oh?"

"How do you take your coffee?"

"I . . . You're feeding me?"

"I'm not going to have you dying of starvation out in the middle of the field today. A full day's work requires a full stomach."

"Oh," she said again.

"You can sit at the kitchen island, there. I don't really have a dining table."

"Oh. Sure."

She sat at the island, plate in front of her, and her stomach growled viciously.

She hadn't had any dinner last night. She dug into the eggs enthusiastically.

"Birdie," he said. "Coffee?"

"I don't care how you fix it. I like it anyway I can get it."

"Come on now, you have to have a preference."

"I don't know. How do you drink it?"

"I usually put in a little bit of half-and-half and a spoonful of sugar."

"Really? You seem like the kind of guy who would drink it black and growl about how tough you are."

"Nah, Birdie, I'll let you in on a little secret. If a man ever has to tell you how tough he is, he's not. And especially if he has to tell you he's tough because he has a drink a certain way."

She huffed a laugh. "Okay. You can fix mine the way you do yours."

That was usually what she did. If she was bunking down with a guy, she let him choose how to make coffee. Seemed reasonable. Sometimes it was black, sometimes just cream. Sometimes overly sweet. Sometimes not sweet enough. But beggars couldn't be choosers, or something like that.

"All right."

He poured a generous amount of coffee into a mug, then some cream and sugar. He passed it to her, and she took a sip. It was a little bit too light and too sweet for her, but it didn't matter. It was going to do the job. And she was pleased.

Before she fully emptied her plate, he piled more bacon and more eggs onto it, and she ate every last bite. She sat there for a moment, nearly humming with pleasure.

She couldn't remember the last time she'd been this full. It was wonderful.

"Another coffee for the road?" She looked up at him and was nearly surprised that he was the same Gunnar Parsons who had railroaded her last night. Surprised he was the same Gunnar Parsons she had known all her life—inflexible, morally superior, and a general pain in the ass.

He was being so . . . almost nice. Except, he was forcing her to work on his ranch.

She was having a hard time finding any animosity toward him, though.

"Sure," she said.

He poured some coffee into a to-go cup, and then she followed him out the front door to his truck.

"You're staying on the family ranch?"

"Yeah. But if I were you, I would drive in as near as you can to the back, and then let me walk across the field to the barn where my stuff is. I don't want to see my dad, and I'm sure you don't either."

"I'm not scared of your dad."

Birdie huffed. "I'm not scared of him. My God. He's probably drunk off his ass, if he's up. More than likely he's passed out. I just don't want to deal with him."

"All right."

He followed her directions and drove to the edge of the

property. "If I'm not back in five minutes . . . Well, don't call the cops."

"I'm going with you," he said, turning the engine off and getting out of the truck.

"You don't need to do that."

"I'm going to come with you, Birdie. So stop making an issue. Let's just go get your stuff."

She hissed and complained the whole way across the field, about the weeds, which thankfully were not in her socks, and about his presence. Because it was unnecessary. She really didn't understand why he was doing all this. From feeding her to making sure she had backup for the trip to the barn. Not that she needed it.

"I sneak in this way," she said, wiggling a board out of its place and slipping through.

"God Almighty," he muttered as he squeezed in behind her, working much harder than she had to get his muscular frame through the opening.

She hurried over to the corner, grabbed her backpack and her rolled-up sleeping bag. She'd made sure all of her things were packed and ready to go before she'd headed out to Gunnar's last night. It just made sense to always be ready to run.

"This is all I have," she said.

He looked at the bag, at the sleeping bag, then back at her. She wished he was disdainful. She wished he was looking at her the way he had last night. Because thinking she was beneath him was one thing; looking at her with pity was quite another.

She never liked it. Not if the person was a middle-aged church lady, or a purple-haired activist. But she especially didn't like it from an extremely good-looking man.

"I like to travel light," she said. "Now let's get out of here."

She led the way, slipping back through the opening and making sure to comment on the fact that she hadn't needed him to go with her.

Right then, he grabbed the back of her backpack and pulled it off her.

"Maybe you didn't need me."

As the straps of the backpack dragged down over her arms, she was forced to drop her sleeping bag. "That wasn't helpful," she said, picking it up and brushing it off. "Now there's probably stuff stuck to it. I hate that."

"Well, you don't need it right at this moment."

"It's the only sleeping bag I have," she said. "And I will need it at some point. I'm not staying up in a room in your barn forever."

"Point taken." He took the sleeping bag out of her arms. "I'm just going to carry your things. Maybe you didn't need me. Sorry I made you drop your sleeping bag. I just thought I would help."

"But why?" she asked, now walking behind him as he strode purposefully ahead. "I don't get it. You don't even like me. Is this some kind of good guy complex? A hero thing? I don't need you to be a hero. Much less my hero. Do you know what, Gunnar? I'm my own hero. I always have been."

"I'm not trying to be your hero. I'm just trying to not be an asshole."

"Does that take a concerted effort?"

"Sometimes," he said.

"Not as far as I can tell. You're just so good. You always have been. I found that annoying even when we were kids. One time I jumped out of a tree in front of the school and scared Ethan Mobley half to death, and you picked him up and said that I was mean. And it was mean. But it was funny."

"Is it really funny if somebody else is afraid?"

"I was a tiny girl—it's not like I was going to actually hurt him."

"Well, he didn't know that. And in the moment, he was scared."

She wrinkled her nose. "I don't feel bad about it. Still. My point stands. You're just a natural do-gooder. It's in your DNA. And I guess I'm naturally bad. It's just in mine."

"I don't believe in any such thing," he said. "I don't believe that people are born good or born bad." He shrugged. "Hell. I figure the call on whether or not you're good or bad isn't even set until you're dead."

"Disagree. I think if you're a serial killer, you're a bad person."

"Well, what if you are, and then you experience a change and you save more people than you ever killed?"

She shrugged. "I still think you're bad."

"So if a person makes a mistake, they're just human garbage?"

"To be fair, Gunnar, a mistake is accidentally washing your white socks with the colored socks and making them dingy. Being a serial killer isn't really a mistake."

"So you think there's a certain point that no one can come back from?"

"I'm not getting into religion or philosophy here. Maybe there's a chance for you to redeem your eternal soul. But on earth, you're a piece of garbage."

"That's interesting. Not what I expected from somebody with your rather elastic version of morality."

She shrugged. "Many people would argue that I'm a piece of garbage."

"I would never say that about you."

"Of course not. Because you're a good guy. I rest my case."

"There's no resting your case. If I stopped being decent now, I would think that none of the good I did before would matter. You have to think it can go the other way."

"Is this a roundabout way of trying to tell me that I can still see the light?"

142 / *Maisey Yates*

He shook his head. "No. I wouldn't dream of telling you that."

Truthfully, she didn't know whether or not to be offended.

She opted for offended, because otherwise she was beginning to feel a little bit warm toward him, and she didn't like that at all. When they arrived at the truck, she got inside quickly and immediately grabbed her things back from him. He didn't say anything but just started the truck and began the return drive to the Parsons ranch.

He pulled up in front of the barn, and she got out, making her way to her temporary bedroom, where she took her things upstairs. Thankfully, there was a very small bathroom in the apartment, and also a shower. She would be able to get clean later, which she very much appreciated. But for now, there was work.

She went back down the stairs and found him still waiting in his truck. She got back inside. "What are we doing today?"

"I've got to hitch the excavator up to the back of the truck, and then I'm towing it out to one of the far fields. We're going to be doing a little bit of leveling. And I need you to shovel the dirt into the back of the truck. Because we're going to be using it to fill in some low places. That's basically the job. Shaving off the high places, filling up the low ones."

"Very technical," she said.

She had no idea what he meant by hitching the excavator up but soon learned when they pulled up to a small tractor that sat on a flatbed trailer. He backed the truck up to it with great skill, then got out of the vehicle and attached the flatbed to the ball hitch.

She clapped when he got back in, and he treated her to a scathing look.

She grinned.

She was no longer grinning when they arrived at the field and she caught a glimpse of how big a job it was going to be.

"Why can't I drive the tractor?"

"Because you're a menace."

"Well. Well." She was going to say something argumentative, because again, she was very good at that. But he wasn't wrong.

"Do you know how to drive a tractor?"

She laughed. "No. But it can't be that difficult. I taught myself how to do everything I know how to do. Why couldn't I teach myself to drive a tractor? I drive other things."

He shook his head. "You have an outsized sense of self-confidence—has anyone ever told you that?"

She laughed. "I have to. Nobody else has any confidence in me. I have to believe in myself. Otherwise, I wouldn't do anything."

He looked at her for a long moment. "It's true," she continued. "I know you don't approve of all the things I've done to survive. Particularly the whole stealing from you thing. Fair. I get it. But . . . I have to live. I'm not going to have a terrible life just because my dad sucks. Can you think of anything dumber than that? He doesn't get to decide how happy I'm going to be."

"That's fair. But you still aren't driving the tractor." He reached into the back of the truck and grabbed hold of a shovel, thrusting it toward her. "Pretty soon you're going to have a whole lot of dirt to move. You'll probably want to drive the truck up to the pile and then shovel it in."

"This seems inefficient."

"Oh well," he said.

Then he got into the really cool tractor and started moving dirt around.

Soon enough there was a pile large enough for her to begin loading up the truck. She got inside, grabbed the keys and started up the engine, driving it over to the dirt pile before getting out and taking up her shovel again.

She began to make small inroads, lifting one shovelful at a time into the back of the truck.

Her shoulders were aching. And it took a couple of hours for her to fill the truck. But by the time it was ready, he came back over, shut the tailgate and nodded. "Great work. Now we can take the dirt and spread it out down below."

"Can't I just give you a blow job?" She was sweaty and unhappy. This was taking a lot longer than sexual favors would.

He frowned. "Do men really treat you like that?"

"Like what?"

"This isn't the first time you've acted like it would be just as reasonable for me to ask you to . . . to do something like that." He was trying to be delicate. It was almost sweet. Except nothing about Gunnar really read *sweet*.

"Yes. Of course they do. That's what makes the world go round. That's what men want." She felt ridiculous standing there, looking up at a man and trying to explain to him what men wanted. Surely, he already knew.

"That's what terrible men want. No real man would ever put a woman in that position. Where she felt she had to trade her body for anything."

She felt dumbfounded by that.

"It's just the way things are," she said. "You don't get anything for nothing. And I'm not talking about, I don't know, official sex workers, not that there's anything wrong with that, I don't judge anyone for doing anything they need to do to get by. But I just mean every relationship is a transaction."

"I guess you could think of it that way if you want. But that's not the case. Sometimes someone gives more; sometimes they get more. Relationships are ecosystems, they aren't cash registers."

She scrunched up her nose. "What the hell does that mean?"

"I mean . . ." He gestured around them, to the craggy blue mountains, the dark green pines, the green and yellow grass, and scattered patches of black and red lava rock. "A long time ago, the mountains here erupted. That lava flow took out a whole lot of nature. Animals, plants. But what happened later? It formed all this mineral-rich soil. All the stuff that's good for growing. So now the trees are strong and tall, and the animals have a lot of food. It's not a system of trading. It's the way one piece supports the other. Without one, the other doesn't exist. They each contribute essential pieces of themselves to the land. The animals eat the grass, and then they die and become part of it."

"And that," she said, holding her arms out dramatically, "is the circle of life."

He sighed heavily, and she felt a little bit guilty for deliberately brushing past his point. "I just mean, it's not . . . You give your body, a guy gives you . . . what?"

"Bacon and eggs? Coffee? A place to stay for a while. Honestly, there are worse things. It's not as if I didn't like them." But the truth was, she'd never been with a man and imagined herself having a future with him. She hadn't loved any of them.

But sometimes, it was nice to have a soft place to land. Some arms to hold you.

"Well, I don't think that's right. That's not how men should treat you."

"I treat myself that way." The minute the words left her mouth, they made her feel sad. She didn't like that. The only thing she hated more than other people pitying her, was her pitying herself. Because it was pointless, and it didn't gain her anything.

"That's not what we're doing here, okay?"

Maybe he wasn't attracted to her.

A small pang hit her in the stomach. Why did that matter? Sure, he was basically the most beautiful man she'd ever seen, but he was also a pain in the butt. She didn't need him to find her attractive. Not in the least.

"So how do your relationships work then? You are the mountains, and she is the river?"

"No," he said, snorting. "I've never had a . . . very functional long-term relationship, to be honest."

"Then what makes you so sure about how they work?"

He cleared his throat and rested his hand on the rail of the truck bed. "Because when my mom died, it was obvious to me my dad lost something essential. I think she was the river. And after that, he was just a mountain, standing alone. Unable to move, unable to bend. There was plenty he couldn't do for himself. And . . . yeah. I've just seen it. What it's like when an essential piece gets taken away. You never find your way back to yourself after that."

She felt as if she'd been struck. She knew, of course, that his mother had died. That his younger sister had died then too. She just didn't remember it. But it was something people talked about. Still, for her, just the two of them living over at the Parsons ranch was . . . normal.

And then his dad had died a year ago.

Gunnar was alone.

Was he the mountain? Maybe a pine. Left standing out there all alone, with nothing to support him. She had always believed that he had things easy, but now she had to wonder if her vision was a little bit blurry when it came to him.

"Sorry," she said. "That . . . that's rough. About your dad, I mean. I don't know what that's like. Seeing someone change like that. My dad never changes. He's just the same. Always. No person ever made him better or worse. Not a wife, and certainly not me. I've just never seen people be so important to each other."

"I like to think they can be. And until I find something like that, I don't want it." He let out a harsh breath. "Mostly, though, I don't want it. It just looks like it hurts."

She nodded slowly. "I get why you think some of the decisions I've made seem sad, or maybe like somebody was taking advantage of me. Maybe they were, but I've never felt that way. It's been all right. And I don't get hurt. I never want to love someone more than they love me, right? So . . . stuff like that, it's fine. It's companionship, anyway."

"Well, I don't require that kind of companionship from you. Okay? This isn't charity, anyway. I'm not being that nice to you."

She blinked. "You fed me."

"That's the bare minimum, Birdie. People should feed you."

And with that, the conversation was sort of over. They drove down to the other side of the field, and he helped her get the dirt out and spread it over the lower parts of the field.

She kept thinking about what he'd said. That he wasn't being nice to her.

She was listing all the things he had done, and every one of them seemed pretty nice.

She thought maybe he didn't know how nice.

They got back into the truck and drove back toward the excavator, because they were going to do another round of this nonsense. "You are nice," she insisted.

"I didn't think you liked me."

"I don't," she said, though the denial felt a little bit less authentic than it had yesterday. "But whether or not I like you has nothing to do with whether or not you're being nice."

"I just think people ought to take care of each other. Okay? Especially when they're your neighbor. And I guess I didn't realize how . . . I didn't realize you were living in a barn. I didn't realize you were that desperate. Yeah, I was mad when you came and stole my horse. I'm not going to make you pay anything back now. I'm just going to pay you. For all the work you're doing here."

She was stunned. "But I . . ."

"My dad held on to a lot of resentment against your dad.

But you're not him. And I'm not going to hold what he did against you."

"Well, that's . . ."

"It's just decent. Okay, tonight you're eating dinner with me too, and you're not going to argue about it."

She snorted. "I've never turned down a free meal in my life."

But privately, she felt this was all a little bit much, and she wondered when the other hay-filled sock was going to drop.

Chapter 4

He didn't quite know what to make of Birdie after that whole long day of work. She wasn't quite the same as he had imagined her to be.

But then, he could honestly admit that he hadn't imagined her to be anything like a real person.

She was an emblem, because his dad had always said that her family was a bushel of bad apples. But she wasn't . . . She wasn't bad. She was scrappy. She was strange. Sad, even, in some ways. He felt bad for her. That was what surprised him most. He hadn't expected to ever feel a lick of pity for Birdie Lennox. And here he was, about to grill her some steak.

He brought a plateful of steaks outside, and put them on his hot, flattop grill. Birdie had gone back to the apartment to take a shower, and it was his first break from her all day.

He would've thought it would be a good thing to get away from her. But he sort of missed the chatter.

He couldn't remember the last time he'd had a conversation like that with someone. He tossed the first steak on the grill, and it sizzled. No. He'd never had such an intense conversation with anyone. Ever. His dad just didn't talk, and . . . he couldn't even really remember his mom's voice anymore.

He could still remember some of his sister's baby talk. He didn't like to, though. It made his heart feel as if it was too large for his chest. He would never characterize himself as lonely. He had this place. He had business contacts—he made conversation frequently with the farrier who did shoes for his horses, with the guys who delivered hay and feed. But being with Birdie for part of the day made him feel . . . something different. It made him feel like maybe there was something he was missing. He couldn't quite put a finger on it.

"Lord Almighty." He turned and saw Birdie jogging toward him. Her copper hair was in a ponytail, swinging behind her, and she was wearing a light blue T-shirt, and a pair of short pink shorts. She looked . . . carefree in a way he couldn't say he'd seen her before.

"Evening," he said.

"No way. Steak."

"Yes. I have a cattle ranch."

"That is way above my pay grade. Not that I'm complaining."

"Can you get yourself into the house and grab the corn on the cob that's sitting on the counter?"

She looked a little bit surprised but didn't admit it. Instead, she wordlessly went up the stairs and into the house, returning a few moments later with a tray laden with corn on the cob.

"Give it here," he said.

Her ponytail was swinging wildly as she hop-stepped over to him.

He took out his tongs and put the corn on the griddle, right on top of some melted butter, and he could practically see hearts in Birdie's eyes.

"This is a treat," she said.

"Well, you deserve it after putting in a full day's work like that."

"I'm not afraid of hard work, you know."

"I've gathered that."

"It's just, nobody trusts my dad, and they shouldn't. They also don't trust me. And I guess they shouldn't."

She frowned.

"Well, it's not too late for you to try to actually get to know some people in town and make sure they know who you really are."

"I don't want do that. I want to leave. What's the point of being named after a bird if you can't use your wings to fly?"

For some reason, the idea of Birdie Lennox not being around anymore made him unaccountably sad. It shouldn't. He had decided she was a menace long ago. He had decided she was a nonsensical, useless termagant, in fact. There was really no reason to be sad thinking about a world she wasn't in.

"I've never even thought about leaving," he said.

"Why not?"

The answer sat heavy in the center of his chest, and he almost didn't want to say it. But he didn't see the point of lying, either. He had already told Birdie some things that he had never told anybody else. So why not tell her this too?

"My whole family is buried here. I can't really imagine leaving."

A little crease appeared between her fine, rust-colored brows. "Oh. I never thought of that. That's . . . that's really sad."

"It is," he said, his voice gruff. "I just can't imagine leaving them. I'm the only one left. If I don't bring them flowers and all of that . . . there's nobody else to do it."

And the truth of the matter was, once he was laid to rest beside his family, there would be no one left.

But he had never thought about having kids, having a wife.

He had seen what the loss had done to his dad.

And he didn't think he could do what his father had done. Shove it all down, swallow down the pain with whiskey at night.

No. He didn't think . . .

It just wasn't in him. So he wouldn't do it.

But that made for an awfully lonely picture. But maybe that was how it should be. His mother gone way before her time, his sister gone before she could ever become the person she was supposed to be. It was that ecosystem again. Maybe he and his dad had never gotten the nutrients they needed after that. Maybe they were just destined to die off.

"What?" Birdie asked, breaking into his thoughts.

"Just thinking. So, you're going to leave?"

"Yep. I was going to Texas. I had a ride over there, though I guess I have to text him and let him know I can't make it. Unless I decide to steal your horse in the middle of the night."

He looked at her, and he honestly couldn't tell if she was kidding or not. "Are you for real?"

"No. I'm not going to take your horse. I . . . listen, you're not so bad."

"I'm not so bad?"

"Yeah. I always thought that you believed you were better than everybody else. I thought you were holier than thou, you know? And you kind of are. But the thing is, you mean it. You aren't just acting that way because you want to prove you're better than somebody else. You might actually be better than other people. At least, nobody's ever been better to me."

He was lanced with guilt. Because he didn't think he had been all that nice to her, actually. He had essentially taken her captive. He had practically put her in prison above his barn.

She just thought he was being nice because he'd given her coffee and eggs. But that was such a low bar. She should expect better than that. She should get better than that.

"Birdie, the way I see it, you can't help the family you were born into. And sure, you've gotten up to your fair share of shenanigans . . ."

"Is this where you tell me it's not fair for me to be punished for the sins of my father? Because the truth is, I've committed a lot of my own. I'm not eighteen; I'm twenty-eight. A lot of my reputation is earned. And I can deal with that. It's why I want to leave, actually. Because it's not just that people in town don't like me, or think I'm a menace, though that is true. It's that if I don't change my surroundings, *I'm* never going to change. It's not that I'm trying to cut corners. It's not that I want to take the easy way. But I feel like I don't have anything here. I'm just rolling a boulder up the hill, endlessly. And I'm never going to make it to the top. Just going to roll down and have to start all over again. And you know, there's a point where you begin to feel tired." She let out a sigh, and her slim shoulders shifted. "That's when you start debating whether or not you can afford morality. You have lots of horses, I don't have any. I couldn't see another way to get to Texas. And so taking yours started to seem right in my head. It started to make sense."

"Do you want to go to Texas?"

Suddenly, he wanted to offer to send her there.

She shook her head slowly. "I think . . . if it's all right with you, I think I'll keep this job. I don't know what kind of man I'm going to find in Texas. And I don't know what my ride is going to ask for along the way. But I already know that you're not . . ."

His chest burned. The idea that men had done that to her, made her feel she had to give them a part of herself in exchange for basic needs, it killed him.

"I wouldn't do that," he said.

She looked up at him, and she smiled. The sun hit her just so, highlighting the very faint freckles sprinkled over the bridge of her nose.

She was very pretty, was Birdie. But no matter how pretty he thought she was, he wasn't going to take advantage of her the way those other guys had done. Not ever.

The very idea enraged him.

His dad had said one time that the world could take everything from you—but it couldn't take away your morals. Sometimes just being good and decent was all you had left.

He was going to be good and decent.

It didn't matter how pretty she was. Hell, treating a woman like that had nothing to do with how pretty she was. Nothing to do with what she was wearing. It had everything to do with a man feeling so small that he wanted to feel powerful by proving that he could get something through manipulation.

Gunnar wanted nothing to do with that behavior.

"You got a safe place here, I promise you that. For as long as you want it."

"Even if it's longer than the two months?"

"Even if it's longer. I want to help you get on your feet."

"That's . . . that's the nicest thing anyone has ever said to me. Honestly."

He took all the food off the grill and put it onto a big tray. Then he gestured for her to follow him to a picnic table down in front of his porch.

He set the food in the center of the table, then went back inside for a couple of plates, and two bottles of beer.

He brought it all out and set it in front of her. Birdie dug into the food before he even sat down.

She was half feral. And though he had always known that, he didn't think he had ever really known it. He had sort of had this vague thought about bad seeds. His dad had put that thought in his head. Because his dad's version of right and wrong was so rigid.

He didn't look at people who did questionable things and try to understand them.

Gunnar did, though. He wanted to know what had brought someone to that point.

And in the case of Birdie, it was pretty clear to him that she had been dealt a bad hand.

But she had a great attitude. She was sharp and funny; she

was resilient. She was living in tragic circumstances, and yet there was never a note of self-pity in her voice.

She was buoyant in a way he had never seen before.

Yeah, his dad had been good. And he had also been absolutely wrecked by his circumstances.

Not that losing a wife and a child was the same as growing up with a generally bad father, but . . .

"Thanks so much for the food," she said. "It's been slim pickings lately."

"Yeah?"

"The thing is, I keep trying new ventures, and then they fall apart. I've invested in different businesses, different friendships, different relationships, and when they fall apart, there's nothing left. The most recent implosion was me working for a dispatch company, helping arrange freight loads for truckers. I was subcontracted to do the work, and then my boss . . . He started asking for sexual favors. Like I said, I don't really mind . . . I don't know, I've lived with guys before, and I knew I wasn't in love with them, and I knew it wasn't going to be forever. But I'm not flat out paying to keep a job by sucking some guy's dick. He was married and everything . . . And I don't like that. The thing is, I don't like liars."

"You lied to me when I caught you stealing my horse," he said, barely managing to get the words past the rage that was burning in his chest. Not at her, but at the guy that would take advantage of someone like her.

"Well yeah, but that's different. He had everything—a house, somebody who loved him, someone who married him, had kids with him. I don't . . . I don't understand how he could act that way. You know? I think maybe that's why I respect you. Because the truth is, you have a lot of good things, but you seem to do your best to treat everybody with respect. If all you have is garbage, and you roll it downhill, I guess I can understand that. But if you got good things, and you're still rolling garbage downhill . . ."

"That's a good point," he said.

"Well, it's just how I see it. That's all."

"I think my dad was kind of an alcoholic," he said. "But he only hurt himself. And I never would've said he was an alcoholic. But then he died of liver failure. And it was clear that I had missed a lot. He was just so functional. He always did good things. He wasn't someone who was stealing from people in the middle of an addiction or anything like that. He was just stoic, always. And I remember at night I would see him drink his whiskey, but I wasn't keeping track of how much. I wonder if I failed him."

"Well, that's just not fair," Birdie said. "Because my dad is positively pickled in alcohol, and you would think it would've killed him by now. He's a notorious drunk. And he's no good to anybody. It's not fair that drink killed your dad before it killed mine."

"Well. Thanks. But I think that's probably just . . . life. It wasn't really fair that my mom and my sister died when they did. And in the end, my dad died because of that car crash too, just twenty-four years later."

She blinked. "Yeah. I guess so. That's one way of looking at it."

"It is."

"Your sister would have been my age."

"Yeah. I guess she was."

"I wonder if we would've been friends."

"I don't think so. My dad probably wouldn't have let her."

Birdie nodded. "Yeah. I guess so, but I'm pretty persistent. And I probably would have been sneaky. I think I would've liked playing with her."

Her eyes shimmered with tears, and the sight shocked him. Because she didn't seem like a very emotional person, and yet there she was, nearly crying at the memory of his sister, which he couldn't even do.

"There's just so much that's not fair, and I don't usually waste my time thinking about it," she said. "Because what can you do? You can't do a damn thing, can you? Life just isn't fair. And so you go on. But I got to live. All these years. And your sister didn't. There's a whole lot of unfair that I'm used to, but not that. I never even thought about it. I just always thought about how you had it so much better than me. And you didn't. It was hard over here too."

"My dad was a good man," he said. "He was good to me."

"No, I know that. But it's easy to let yourself think that because somebody is comfortable, physically, they don't know the kind of pain you know. I just thought . . . I just thought you could afford to worry about all these little things, like trespassing, because you had stuff. Because you had a good dad."

"It's not a competition, actually. My dad and I went through some loss. But it doesn't mean your life wasn't hard."

She sniffed. "Well, I'm just sorry."

"That means a lot. Especially coming from you." He meant it.

The two of them had never connected on a personal level. Now suddenly it seemed . . . very personal.

"Why were you upset about your socks?"

It was an off-topic question, but something he'd been thinking of since he had snagged her off the road.

"What you mean?"

"I just mean . . . you were really specifically upset about your socks."

"They were gritty," she said, "because I ran to the field barefoot, because I didn't want to make any noise, but in the stable they got full of hay. And I really hate that feeling. Honestly, I can be uncomfortable in so many ways, but trapped dirt and grit drives me crazy. Sand in your sleeping bag, gritty stuff in your shoes—I can't take it."

He had never really heard her complain. And this was a full-throated complaint. "That seems like a small thing to be so furious about."

"Sometimes you have to sweat the small things. Or the big things overwhelm you."

"I guess that's true."

"It's very true. It's sort of therapeutic. You let yourself get really annoyed by something that is the opposite of world ending, and then when the big things come your way, you can cope."

"I'll have to take your word for it."

She took a second steak. "This is great."

He didn't quite know what to make of this woman. This woman who was half feral and all fascinating.

This woman who had been treated so roughly by the world.

Who would she have been if life had treated her a little bit softer?

His dad never would've asked that question, but maybe he should have. Because Gunnar wondered who his dad would've been if he hadn't lost the love of his life. If he hadn't lost his little girl. Who would he have been? Would he have been able to express his feelings? Would he have drunk so much?

Could something have stopped his drinking? That was what really haunted Gunnar.

It seemed to him that Birdie was trying to change gears. That she was trying to remedy some of the crap put on her by her dad. Good for her.

"Well, one of the benefits of your new job is clean socks."

"Don't make promises you can't deliver on." She attacked that second steak with relish and cleared the plate in only a few bites.

"This isn't some empty promise. It's a guarantee."

"No one's ever made me a guarantee before. Well, not one that I trusted."

"I've never had anyone to make one to."

"Well, I'm going to hold you to it. I expect a package of new socks by the end of the week."

"Great. Make sure you're at the house tomorrow by seven for coffee and breakfast. I don't want you fainting in the field."

"I don't faint. That's for mere mortals. I transcend."

With that, she swallowed the rest of her beer, stood up from the table, turned around and walked off.

It was going to be interesting working with her.

And he had a feeling the interesting part was only just starting.

Chapter 5

She'd had a full week's work with Gunnar Parsons, and it had been . . . way nicer than she would like to admit. He always fed her. He said it was part of her pay. She thought it was above and beyond. And during those meals, she always learned a little bit more about him. He was . . . fascinating.

He was gorgeous and handsome and hot, and in some ways seemed too good to be true. As if he was made up by a woman, or something. Except he was thirty years old and hadn't had a long-term relationship of any kind. Not that she had, but she didn't present as emotionally well-adjusted.

It made her wonder if there was something a little bit wrong with him.

But if so, she hadn't seen it.

She showed up at the house that morning bright and early at seven o'clock, and she didn't even bother to knock, because he just expected her at this point. When she walked in, he was standing at the island, with four cups of coffee in front of him.

"What's that?"

"I have here four completely unadulterated cups of coffee. I want you to fix your own coffee, do some taste tests and decide what you like."

"What?"

"I noticed that you drink what I drink, but I'm not convinced that's what you like."

"Well, that's dumb," she said.

It was kind of true. Though she could honestly say that now Gunnar Coffee was always going to be a little bit sentimental for her because she was enjoying her time working with him.

A lot. More than she wanted to admit.

"Is it dumb? Because you don't seem to like it very much. You just take what I take. And the last couple of days I've messed with it, and you haven't said anything."

Her mouth dropped open. "I thought you were honest."

"I'm flexible on certain things. And I was just curious."

"Oh. Well."

"I want you to figure out what you like. You don't have to drink charity coffee. You are a full-fledged member of this household. Part of my team. And it matters what you want."

Her heart thundered painfully in her chest. The things he said made her feel . . . Well, she didn't want to think about what they made her feel. She had no business feeling that way. She . . .

She couldn't go catching feelings for this man.

This man who had lived next door to her basically all her life and had always disdained her on some level or another. She couldn't catch feelings for him. It would just be silly.

She had never felt . . .

She cleared her throat. "Okay. If I do that, will you lay off?"

"Maybe."

She made a hissing sound, just to put him off balance, then walked over to the counter. There was a sugar bowl, a pitcher of cream, some milk, and some vanilla flavoring, which she opened and sniffed delicately.

"Well, I don't know where to start."

"Why don't you taste it plain?"

She picked up the cup and sipped it gingerly. She made a face. "No. Not plain. Please."

He chuckled. Then he handed her the sugar bowl. She took a spoon, and measured carefully, then put a little bit of cream on top of that. She stirred it around and tasted it. It was okay. Not terrible.

But a little bit too sweet.

She went to the next cup, put in just a little bit less sugar, added just a little bit less cream.

She tasted it and added a bit more of each. But then it was too much.

She made a scoffing sound.

"Try the third one."

She did, and this time she managed to get it just right. A little bit less sugar than he used, a little bit more cream. But not as much she had done on cup number two.

"Perfect," she said.

"Well there. Now you know just how you like your coffee. And you don't need to drink it the way I drink it. You can drink it the way you want."

"Well, I guess so," she said.

She couldn't understand, not for the life of her, why he had done this for her. Why he had taken the time out of his day for her?

And he had thought of it while she wasn't even here. He had done this for her without her asking. He had thought of her when she wasn't in the room.

She thought about Gunnar quite a bit at this point, sometimes even when she was in the shower, but to know that he thought about her when she wasn't there . . . That was something else.

"Thank you," she said. "For doing that for me." Because it

wasn't going to kill her to be nice. Nobody had ever taught her that. One time, a teacher at school had told her that it didn't cost anything to be kind. She'd told her dad, and he'd said it didn't cost anything to be mean either.

That had stuck with her, and she supposed it wasn't a great thing that it was her father's lesson that she had internalized.

Maybe it was inevitable. The sins of the father, etc., etc.

No one ever said daughters inherited those things, but times had changed. Girls could inherit things now.

"Yeah. Well. You've been doing good work around here."

"I'm glad you think so. I mean, I'm glad I'm not dead weight."

"Actually, I have to go to town today and get some supplies at the Farm and Garden. Would you like to come?"

"Would you invite just any ranch hand?"

She didn't know why she suddenly felt so desperate to feel special. Except that it would be very nice to be special to somebody like Gunnar.

Just thinking about it made her feel warm. She shouldn't be thinking things like that.

Speaking of things she couldn't afford. The love of a good man was definitely one of them.

She felt her shoulders rise up an inch. Who was talking about love anyway? Certainly not her. She was attracted to him, sure. But who wouldn't be? Honestly, who wouldn't be. He was an incredibly handsome man. Well over six feet, broad shouldered, muscular, and he was just so . . .

He was nice, but she didn't have the feeling that it came naturally to him.

It was more that there was a goodness deep inside him, and he acted on that goodness even when it was difficult. He wasn't saccharine, he wasn't sweet, he was something even better.

She thought of what he'd said about the ecosystem. About his father being a mountain.

She thought that Gunnar might be a mountain. It suited him. He was strong. As if he was propping up everything around him. He had said that his dad was a mountain, and he had died from not having what he needed, but what did a mountain need?

She wanted to know. Because she sort of wanted to give it to him. Oh, not like that. She didn't think she had the power to prop up Gunnar Parsons' personal ecosystem. Far from it. He had done so many nice things for her.

"Yeah. Let's go to town."

Which was how she found herself riding shotgun next to Gunnar without really considering whether or not people in town would find it odd that the two of them were together.

Thankfully, she wasn't exactly a regular at the Farm and Garden store, so it wasn't populated with people she knew by sight.

"We might be the talk of the town if the wrong person runs into us," she pointed out.

"I've never been the talk of the town in my life," he said.

"Yes, that's because you don't hang out with baddies," she said, bringing her hands up and making claws with her fingers.

"Is that what you are?"

"According to some. Though some might say that I'm a baddie as in a villain, and some would say I'm a baddie as in very hot." She batted her eyes and him, and he stared at her for a moment. Just a moment longer than he normally would, and his eyes looked just a little bit harder. And she wondered, at least for a second, if he thought she was pretty. No. He was too good for something like that. Too good for her.

She had to be imagining things because . . .

This was the problem. If somebody made you feel special, then you just wanted to keep feeling special. She wasn't special. She was just her. Kind of a no-account born to somebody destined to be forgotten by history.

Definitely not the kind of person Gunnar would ever . . . make eyes at, or anything remotely like that.

She scurried behind him as he went inside the Farm and Garden, not really commenting on what she had said. That was fine. She didn't need him to agree or disagree.

He grabbed a flat cart and picked up a new hose, a roll of barbed wire and some new tools. She saw a bright pink pair of work gloves and looked at them for a moment but didn't linger on them long. He hadn't paid her yet, but she hadn't really needed any money. And she didn't want to ask him, because he was being overly accommodating.

Besides, even if she did have some money, she wouldn't spend it on something like that. It was too frivolous.

"Add the gloves to the cart," he said.

She looked up at him. "What?"

"You heard me. You want them."

"I barely looked at them. How did you even . . ."

"I pay attention to you."

She had nothing to say to that. She just got the gloves and put them on the cart. She didn't know what to say at all, not for the whole rest of the shopping trip. He paid attention to her? What did that even mean?

Chapter 6

When they got back to the truck, she was still mulling over what she was supposed to say about that. When they got in the truck, he handed her the gloves, and she clutched them tightly, pressing them down into her lap.

"Feels like the kind of day to maybe just go for a ride," he said.

"What?"

"Yeah. We've both been working really hard. Don't you think?"

"I guess so. But you know, ranch work is never done and all of that."

"It never is. Which is why sometimes you have to take a break. Not that my dad ever would've thought that."

"He sounds like an interesting guy."

"He was."

She looked down at the gloves and rubbed her thumb over the top of them. She thought about the time Gunnar had touched her hand. Then she swallowed hard, trying to push that memory aside.

"Well, I would love that. If I could ride Pegasus."

"Alfalfa Sprout?"

"I said what I said." She shot him her cheesiest grin.

"Why do you like that name so much?"

"Because Pegasus is just like me. A horse that has wings, and it's going to fly away."

"Still intent on flying away?"

Her eyes caught his, and something felt strange in her chest. She couldn't say that she had ever thought the town of Sisters felt much like home. But there was something about his eyes that felt like home, and as soon as she had that thought, she wanted to push it away. As soon as she had that thought, she wanted to never have it again. Another person couldn't be home. That was ridiculous. And far too much weight to put on another soul.

"She doesn't respond to her name. If you want to call her Pegasus, you can."

Pink gloves and Pegasus. He really was just a little bit too much.

"Why are you being so nice to me?"

"You keep asking me that. You keep acting like you don't deserve decent treatment. Like you aren't worthy of it. Why do you think that?"

"You know why. It's the same reason that you instantly went after me that first day, so don't act like you don't know."

"It took me all of ten minutes to realize there was more to your story than I ever fully realized."

"Well, it's just weird. Because nobody is nice to me. Nobody."

"Well, people are pretty nice to me. Polite, anyway. But I've realized something over the past week. I don't really talk to anybody. I have acquaintances, but I don't have any friends. I thought maybe we were starting to become friends, Birdie."

That word burned through her. She wanted it. She wanted it

desperately. And yet, she also wanted something more. Which was unfair, and completely . . . unimaginable.

Except, she was beginning to imagine it.

But she had to stop.

She wasn't a romantic by nature.

Sure, she liked men. She found them attractive. But there was nothing romantic in that.

Never had been, not for her.

When they got back to the ranch, she squirreled her gloves away in her room, and then met him down at the stable, where he already had the horses prepared to go.

"I packed us some sandwiches."

"You really do think of everything."

"Not naturally. But it's kind of nice to have somebody else to think about. I've been . . . It's been a lonely year."

Hearing him say that, seeing this mountain of a man display a little bit of vulnerability, made her chest feel tight.

"Sorry."

"No need to be sorry. Grief is a little bit too familiar to me. Though I'm used to old grief. I'm used to missing something I can barely remember. It's hard. You know, I think there were a lot of things I should've said to my dad. But I didn't know what they were until it was too late. I didn't realize I was missing certain things until he was gone, and now it's too late."

"That's rough." She meant it.

The corner of his mouth turned up into a smile. "Thanks."

"I've never taken the time to grieve for anything. Or anyone, really. Of course, everyone in my terrible family is still alive, and how fair is that? My mother is off somewhere doing whatever the hell she wants to do, and my father is right next door. For all the good he does me."

He got up on the back of his horse, and she followed suit, mounting up and feeling a sense of freedom as she urged Pegasus forward.

"Just different versions of not having the family we ought to, right?"

"I expect so."

He urged his horse up a narrow trail that was surrounded by thick berry vines and lava rock. She went along after him.

"When did you first realize that you weren't normal?" She had always wondered if other people ever had those sorts of revelations. She had always wondered if she was alone.

"Pardon?" He looked over his shoulder, and her stomach did a little dip as she took in the view of his strong profile, his square jaw, the way that cream-colored cowboy hat cast a shadow over his face. Artful. Just like the landscape itself.

"You know. When did you first realize that your house didn't look like everybody else's."

He made a short sound in the back of his throat. "I can't say that I recall. Just . . . all right, I remember one time when I was in fourth grade I went over to a friend's house, and his mom was there when we got home from school. I'd been over to people's houses before. I'd been to his house, but for some reason her being there and taking our coats and backpacks when we walked in the door . . . I just wondered if all moms did that. I never had before. I'd never wondered. But then I did. And it felt so . . . It hurt, hit me right in the chest. I realized I just didn't have that. And then I started noticing every time I went to someone else's house. The things their moms did. How soft the moms were with them. And my dad could never . . ." His shoulders rose and fell. "That was actually the worst thing. One time after a Little League game, when we lost terribly and were all really upset, one of my friends' dads came over and pulled him in for a big hug. And my friend was crying a little bit but trying not to. His dad comforted him. Mine just . . . stood there. And I knew I could never show sadness that way."

"That sounds really lonely. I'm sorry."

"It was. It's been . . ." He shook his head. "I'm not going to be all self-pitying. I admire your attitude, actually."

"Well, as a defense mechanism, it definitely keeps the momentum going."

"When did you first realize you were weird, Birdie?"

"Oh, a friend of mine invited me over, and about the third time in a row I went over there she said it was rude that I had never invited her to my place. I guess her mom had said it wasn't right that we hadn't invited her over. But I thought about it . . . The idea of my friend coming to my house filled me with a sense of dread. I didn't want her to go over there. Because my house was dirty and messy and my dad was mean. He wasn't going to feed us. Hell, there was probably nothing but beer in the fridge. I wanted to go to her house, where it felt safe and there was something to eat."

"Did you tell her that?"

"No. I told her I didn't want to be her friend anymore, and I never hung out with her again. Because I realized how weird my life was, and I didn't want her to know it. Not ever. So I just got angry. Started a fight. And that was basically . . . formative." She laughed a little bit in spite of herself. "I never met someone I couldn't double down on. That was what I was trying to do when you caught me. I just kept thinking that as long as I didn't let on that I was caught, maybe things could still go my way. I just . . . Fighting to the end, that's what I'm good at. But I'm not good at letting anyone close. Because I could have. I could've told her that my house wasn't a safe place to be. But I would've rather chewed on rocks."

"Yeah, it's hard," he said. "Realizing that your life isn't the same as everybody else's. I'm glad you asked me that, because I hadn't thought about it in a long time. Honestly, I never think about things like that. But it . . . it shapes you, doesn't it? Kind of determines how you're going to live the whole rest of your life. Unless you stop and try to change it."

"Right. And I certainly never did. I just kept on fighting."

She blinked and tried to pay attention to the scenery. At the trees around them, and the way the sunlight filtered through the leaves.

They rounded a curve in the trail and came out of the trees. A whole valley lay right before them, a grand display of striped rocks comprising granite and quartz, with pine trees and lava rock dotting the landscape.

Her breath caught.

"Seems like a good spot to take a break," he said.

He got down from his horse, but she was too busy staring at the view. She didn't notice that he was standing right beside her until he touched her lower back.

She jumped. Electricity skittered up her spine.

She looked down at him, and their eyes caught, and she was sure that she saw that same something she had noticed earlier. That something he had hidden as quickly as it appeared. He didn't hide it quite as quickly this time.

He reached up, hand held out her. "Just going to help you down."

"I can get off the horse myself," she said.

"I'm being a gentleman."

"A gentleman?" She reached her hand out. "Never met one."

Then he wrapped his fingers around hers, and she felt as if she had been struck by a bolt of lightning.

As electric as it had been to make contact with his skin that first night when they'd shaken hands, this was different. The feeling was layered with all the days she had known him now. Not just known of him, not just spoken to him in passing, but really known him.

It felt heavy with the connection they had forged.

It felt . . .

She couldn't breathe.

She started to get down off the horse, and he practically

lifted her with that one hand, keeping her steady until her boots made contact with the ground.

"Oh," she said. She didn't mean to say that. Because it betrayed her. Betrayed the way she felt. The way her heart was galloping in her chest, going this way and that way like an erratic pinball.

He dropped her hand and didn't say anything as he went back to his horse and procured the food that he'd put in the saddlebags.

"I'll just get a blanket laid out," he said.

A blanket, folded neatly in the other side of the saddlebag, came out next, and he spread it over the ground.

It was a little bit rocky, but she made herself comfortable.

He handed her a sandwich, and a can of soda. She took both gratefully.

He was careful not to touch his fingers to hers this time.

She wondered if he'd felt it. That electric connection.

But what did it matter? She was going to leave, and he couldn't.

She thought of those graves he had mentioned earlier. His family.

He was the only one left. He had to stay here. She understood that. His connection to them was deep, and even though their deaths were tragic, in some ways, she envied him.

How could she not? Because he did love his family. And they had loved him. It sounded as if his dad had had a difficult time showing it, but there was also a steadiness to him that had never been present in her own father.

"You're thinking awfully loudly," he commented.

"Nothing. I mean, nothing important. I'm just glad that you brought me out here today. I appreciate it."

"Yeah. You like horses?"

She nodded. "I do. That was one thing . . . Growing up we did have some horses on the ranch. And I loved riding them. I pretty much taught myself how to do it. No one cared enough to make sure I knew how. But it was . . . That was the happiest time. When it was just me on the back of the horse, riding like hell across the ranch. I felt free. I felt like anything was possible. If I'm mad at myself about anything, it's that I didn't take that spirit with me. Yeah, I am resilient. But the truth is, I don't think I tried hard enough to get out of here. I wasted a lot of time. I don't know what I wanted. For this place to feel right? For it to all click. For my dad to stop drinking, for my mom to come home. For someone in the grocery store to smile at me. I guess I just didn't want it all to be for nothing. All these years. I wanted to have that moment, me on the back of the horse on the land here, and I wanted my life to feel like that. It never did. And that's why . . . After the whole thing with my last job, I just decided I needed to get out of here. Because I'm never going to get a fair shake if I don't."

"This is your home."

Her eyes met his, and the words felt far too . . . everything. Because when he said that, she didn't think of the land, she thought of him. And she had this terrible, awful feeling that he was the person she'd been waiting for. The reason.

She pushed that notion aside, because she couldn't afford thinking like that. "I guess. But why here and not somewhere else? My family's not buried here. And even when they are, I don't think I'll go visit. That land my dad owns . . . It's just going to get taken by the bank. It's not going to pass to me. The only thing I'll ever inherit is debt. I wish there was a legacy for me to be hanging on to, but there's not. There just isn't. I guess I'm more of an optimist than I ever wanted to believe. Because something kept me here."

"Something," he said.

His eyes were serious now, and she felt herself being drawn to him. She wanted . . . she wanted to be a different person. She wanted to be a different person in a different time. She wanted to be able to want things that she couldn't want. She wanted to be worthy of him.

And horrifyingly, she felt tears beginning to well up, and she didn't cry. Not ever. It wasn't who she was. She hadn't cried in . . . hell, years. Because there was no point in displays of emotion like that. What was the point?

So instead, she scrambled away from him, and made her way over to the edge of the drop-off. She wrapped her arms around herself and looked at the view below. "It is a beautiful place," she said, a little bit too loudly, something, anything to distract them both from what had just happened. Maybe he wouldn't notice.

"Yeah," he said. "It's beautiful."

She looked behind her, and he was standing there, so close. And he was looking at her. Not at the view.

"Life isn't fair," she said. "And I don't waste a whole lot of time being mad about that. But it just . . . it isn't. It isn't fair."

"True enough."

"It sucks," she said.

He laughed. "Yeah. It does."

"I'm going to leave," she said. "Because this place isn't home. Even if . . . You're a much nicer person than I thought you were. Maybe the nicest that anyone has ever been to me."

"What's going . . ."

"Nothing. Thanks for this afternoon. Really. And the pink gloves. Thank you. That's all. I'm just a little bit overwhelmed."

"Yeah."

And then she ran past him, got on her horse, and galloped like hell.

Chapter 7

He had no idea why she had run from him.

He got on his horse and went after her as quickly as possible. By the time he arrived at the barn she had already put Pegasus away. He took care of his own horse as quickly as possible and then walked up the stairs to her apartment.

He felt . . . he just needed to talk to her. There was a pressure in his chest, and he wasn't used to it. This overflow of emotions.

The problem with her was that she brought all this out in him. She made him feel things, made him think about things, made him put voice to things that had stirred inside him for years, things he'd never known how to talk about.

Because he basically hadn't been allowed to.

His dad had never outright said they couldn't talk about his mother and sister, but Gunnar had known it. Somewhere deep in his heart, he had known that if he ever tried to bring the subject up, there would be issues.

But with her, he could talk about his loss. He could put his feelings into words. He could . . .

She opened the door, her eyes round. "Oh."

"I want to talk to you."

"Okay," she said.

She stepped back, and he moved inside. She was breathing hard, and he had a hard time believing that she was still out of breath from the wild ride back. Her breasts were rising and falling with the motion, and he couldn't help but look.

He was her boss, technically. And he suddenly felt . . . bad. That he had come in here like this, that he had . . .

But she was beautiful. She was so beautiful. That wasn't why he was here. It wasn't.

"I just wanted to make sure you were okay."

"Of course, I am."

"No of course about it. You seemed upset when you rode off. And I need you to know, this last week has been really important to me. You're important to me, and . . ."

She took a step forward, her hands balled into fists, and suddenly she planted them on his chest, flat, and then curled her fingers around his shirt. "Let's not talk."

Then she stretched up on her toes and she kissed him. Wild, hard.

And something ignited inside him. With the fire of a thousand suns. He had never felt desire like this before. Had never felt such need. But then, he had never known the woman he was kissing, not like this. And she had never known him. Yeah, he'd exchanged pleasantries with the women he'd been with, but they hadn't known the things that hurt him. The things that kept him up at night. The things that stole his breath and his joy.

That horrible truth about being the last remaining member of his family, and feeling like he had to stay here as the guardian of the graves forever.

But she did.

And whether or not he was her boss was wiped away with the sweep of her tongue over his lower lip.

Because she was just Birdie Lennox, and he was Gunnar Parsons. Two of the most unlikely people to ever find kinship with each other. To ever kiss.

He wrapped his arm around her waist and held her close to his body, angling his head and taking the kiss deeper, his heart pounding wildly, his whole body revved up.

He wanted her. He couldn't remember wanting someone like this before. Because he hadn't. Had they always been destined for this? He had hated her so much when they were kids, but had he really just been scared of all the freedom she represented?

Had he always thought that if he touched her, the wildness might be contagious?

Because he hadn't been able to afford wildness. She said morality was too expensive, but for him, it was the opposite. He'd had to be good. Because there was nothing else to be. He had had one parent left, one family member left, and goodness was the most important thing to his father. If Gunnar wasn't good, then he would lose everything. He couldn't afford to lose everything.

But here he was kissing Birdie, and it wasn't good. Oh, physically it was. Physically, it was phenomenal. Physically, it was the greatest thing he had ever experienced in his life.

But he was her boss. It was wrong.

He pulled away from her. "I am not holding your job over your head. I would never do that. You don't have to kiss me. You don't have to . . ."

"You know, funnily enough," she said, her voice soft, "you're the first man I never wanted anything from except . . . you." She moved her hand down his chest, and there was a softness to her face that he had never seen before. "Gunnar . . . don't do this because you feel bad for me."

"Hell," he breathed. "I don't . . . That's the furthest thing from my mind. But I don't want you to do this because you think you'll lose something if you don't."

"I'm not good enough for you," she said. "Because I am the kind of woman that's been in those situations and I . . ."

"Hey," he said, gripping her chin and forcing her to look up at him. "That's nonsense, okay? You are good enough. You're . . . hell. You're better than good enough. You're the most interesting, resilient, fascinating woman I've ever known. You're the only person I've ever been able to tell all these things to."

"And I'm still leaving," she said. "I'm never going to be anyone's forever, and I get that you can't leave. It's good. I wouldn't even ask you to. But I've never just wanted someone before. And I just want you. That's why I ran away. Because it scared me. Because it's too big. Because it's . . . Can you just kiss me again so that I don't have to think about any of this? So that we don't have to talk about it?"

She was sidestepping, trying to run away from the things they really needed to talk about, but she was so . . . He understood what she was saying. This felt different.

He had been trying to push her away. He had been trying to pretend that he didn't feel it, because he didn't want to lose the . . . the purity of their connection, but now that they were actually standing here, acknowledging the attraction between them, nothing felt less pure. Yet it all felt better. More magical.

Because to have what they had, and to have this too was . . . electric in a way he had never imagined it could be.

Connection.

That was what sex had been missing all this time for him.

Knowing someone.

Except, he also had a feeling it wasn't just that. Because it was something about her. Something that made him let his guard down.

He felt raw. Felt as if she could reach out and touch his heart if she wanted to.

It felt so dangerous. So damned dangerous.

And when he kissed her again, he felt lost.

He couldn't think of a single good reason why he shouldn't kiss her and keep on kissing her.

He wanted to make her feel beautiful. He wanted to give her everything. He wanted to move this so far away from the other experiences she'd had that she would never compare them. He wanted it to be about her.

Giving, not taking.

That was a fantasy he'd never realized he had. But suddenly he was consumed with it.

He kissed her, her lips, her cheek, down her neck.

"I'm going to take care of you," he whispered. "It's going to be good."

His whispered promise sent a cascade of anticipation through her. She knew it was going to be good, because she had never felt anything like this before. She should be relieved, because she wasn't just standing there feeling overwhelmed by emotions anymore. At least this part should be familiar. Kissing. Sex. She knew about a man's body. And she wasn't embarrassed for a man to see hers. But somehow this was different. Somehow, kissing Gunnar hadn't obliterated the emotions inside her.

Suddenly, Gunnar was looking at her as if he wanted to devour her, and she didn't see that upright, Captain America sort of guy she always did when she looked at him. There was something more to him.

Something a little bit wicked, and she had never imagined how much she would like the look of it on him.

He was human. And that wasn't a disappointing thing to realize. It was electrifying. It was everything.

Suddenly, she found herself being lifted off the floor, deposited in the center of the bed.

He was looming over her, and anticipation was building within her.

He pressed his hands down on the mattress on either side of her and kissed her deep, then reached behind his head and pulled his shirt off.

Her breath left her body at the sight of that glorious chest. Had it been only a couple weeks ago that she had first seen him like that, when she had come into the house, and he had given her breakfast? She had been immobilized by how gorgeous he was then, but having him close enough to touch, having him look at her like he wanted her . . .

She felt her throat getting tight again.

Gunnar wanted her.

How was that even possible? How could a good man want her like that?

Because she wasn't good. She wasn't. It had never bothered her until . . . until him. It had never bothered her that she hadn't tried to be good, until she was faced with the best man she had ever known. Now she wanted to be good enough for him, but it was impossible.

Except he wasn't making her feel as if there was something wrong with her. And this felt nothing like a transaction. She reached up and pressed her palm flat against his chest, and her whole body shivered.

She thought she might jitter apart she was shaking so hard.

She moved her hands down that hairy chest, and her toes curled at the erotic sensation, at how hard and hot he was.

With efficient, rough hands, he stripped her T-shirt off her, then reached around and unhooked her bra. She never had been self-conscious about her body, and yet, beneath his intense stare, she found herself worried that she might not be quite what he was after.

"Beautiful," he said. His voice was rough, and he was being honest.

Why had she run from him? From this. When he began to kiss her neck, making his way down to the curve of her breast, she knew. Because it wasn't just pleasure that rioted through her when he took her nipple into his mouth and sucked hard, it wasn't just pleasure she felt when he stripped the rest of her clothes off and put those rough hands between her thighs and began to stroke her.

Her heart hurt. Her whole chest ached. Because he was so impossibly, wonderfully beautiful. Because he was everything that she had ever wanted, that she hadn't even been brave enough to fantasize about.

Was that what had always been between them? At least on her end? Had he hurt to look at because she wanted him to look at her? Had she been angry about how good he was only because she had known that she could never be good enough for him?

Had she wanted him all this time?

Suddenly all the years felt like a waste. All the struggle, all the men.

Everything felt like a waste except this. Except him.

But you're here now.

Yes, but it didn't erase who she was. She was a Lennox. And the Parsons family had always hated the Lennox family.

But he doesn't hate you.

She clung to that, clung to him, held on to his shoulders as he kissed his way down her body, and then settled himself between her thighs. He looked feral.

"I don't . . . No one has ever . . ."

He growled, pressed his mouth where she was most sensitive, where she wanted him most. He licked her, until she was in a frenzy, until she knew nothing other than his name.

And after her climax hit her like a wave, he did it again.

Until she was begging him to stop. Because it was too much. She would never be able to repay him. Not ever.

What if it isn't a transaction? What if he needs it as much as you do? What if he's the mountain and you're the river?

She sobbed his name, but this time it wasn't just from pleasure. It was the desperate sadness of that question inside her. Of her longing that it be true. She longed to be someone who could complete another person. To be something they needed.

But how could she give anything to a man like him?

He was so strong. So solid. And she had tried to steal his horse.

"Hey," he whispered when he moved back to her mouth. He kissed her. "Don't look sad."

"I'm not sad. I am so, so good." She felt bad that she was lying to him, but she didn't want to tell him the truth. Not right now. Not about what she was feeling.

It was too raw. Too personal.

As if what he'd just done wasn't personal . . .

Then he kissed her, deep and sure. She could tell that he was reaching for something, but it didn't matter what. Except then she realized it was a condom, and she realized it mattered quite a lot.

He protected them both and held her while he slid deep inside her.

She had never really understood the way people talked about sex. There was a nice, physical quality to it, sure. But the making love stuff, that had never really resonated. Until now.

Now, she understood. Now, he was holding her as if she was something precious, moving deep within her as if she belonged with him, and that was the single most beautiful experience of her life.

It went beyond pleasure, though there was certainly that too. There certainly was.

She clung to his shoulders and arched against him, shivered as desire took her over.

And the most powerful thing of all was when this mountain of a man trembled with his own pleasure.

He pressed his forehead against hers, kissed her on the mouth, and she realized she didn't want to let him go.

Not for anything. Not for anything in all the world.

When he held her afterward, she didn't have the urge to slip away.

"You should come to the house with me," he said.

She imagined that for a second. Going to sleep in his bed, coming downstairs, having breakfast with him, coffee with him.

Like she belonged. Like it was her place too.

"No," she said. "I shouldn't do that."

"Why not?"

"Because I'm . . . This isn't anything. I know that."

"That's not true," he said. "There's a lot of ground between nothing and forever, you know, Birdie?"

Well, no. She never had.

"You can let me take care of you," he said. "You can let me treat you like something more than . . . I'm very uncomfortable with you being out here. Working here and . . ."

"We've crossed into difficult territory, haven't we?"

"I expect we have, a little bit. Because I still want to make sure that you get what you're owed out of working here, but I need to also be clear that your job isn't contingent on sharing my bed."

"So I could tell you no, and kick you in the butt, and send you right on out of here, and tomorrow you would act like nothing had happened?"

"Yes, ma'am."

"Why?"

"Because I don't treat people like objects. Anyone. But most of all, I care about you, and I'm not going to treat you that way. I understand that you don't want to stay here. I understand that there's no real future for the two of us."

His words hurt more than they should. She didn't want to

184 / Maisey Yates

have a future with him. She didn't want to have a future with anybody. So there.

She was certain of that. She was the one who had said it. So there was no call for her to go feeling upset about it now.

She felt touchy. Testy. Annoyed.

"Right," she said.

Because she was touchy and testy at herself, she had no call to go acting that way toward him.

"I mean it. You can trust me."

"You understand that I've never been able to trust a living soul in this world before."

"Yeah. I do. I also know that sometimes things happen that are beyond people's control. I mean, my mother died, so she didn't get to keep her promises to stay with me. But I know that I have control over whether or not I treat you like you're something to buy. There's no transaction here."

Her stomach felt tight. "Then maybe I'll go inside with you. Maybe I won't kick you in the butt."

"I would appreciate that."

"But what's going to happen in the end?"

He lay on his back, throwing his forearm over his forehead, and stared up at the ceiling. "You know, losing people like I have, I've never thought I had any idea what was going to happen in the end. None of us have control over that. But we can choose what happens along the way. I'd like to walk with you along the way for a little while. What do you think about that?"

It was the single most romantic thing anyone had ever said to her. Honestly. Truly.

She wanted that. To walk a little way with him. Eventually, her path would take her elsewhere. Maybe that was part of the ecosystem thing too, though. Maybe he was a path in her personal woods. Necessary. A journey she had to walk in order to get where she needed to go.

Most of the walking had been hard. Most of it had been almost unbearable. But not this. Not him. He was teaching her that there were different kinds of people than she'd ever encountered before. That men like him existed. Who just wanted to be good because they could be.

She had only ever met men who were bad because they could be.

This was an entirely altering experience.

She took a deep, sore breath. "Yeah. I'd like to go inside."

"Good." He wrapped his arm around her and kissed her temple. And she felt as if she was glowing from the inside out. She got dressed, and so did he, which made her feel slightly mournful, because a man who looked like him should honestly never cover his body up.

Then she went with him downstairs and crossed the open expanse of gravel that led to the ranch house.

"What would your dad say," she said as they walked inside. "Inviting a Lennox to the house."

He looked at her, his eyes intent. "I don't know what he would say, not precisely, but I would tell him that you're one of the best people I've ever known. And that you have every right to be in this house. That you're with me."

Oh, that did make her feel warm and fuzzy in a way that nothing ever had.

She didn't hug herself, but only because she was standing right in front of him, and that seemed a little bit of an embarrassing thing to do.

"All right. That's . . ."

"My dad was a good man. But I've been thinking a lot about how rigid he was in his views. I think I can take goodness and go a little bit further with it. That's what I want, anyway."

"Well, I don't especially want to stretch my dad's meanness."

"You're not. You're stretching your own wings."

Then he lifted her up off the ground as if she weighed nothing and carried her on up the stairs.

And for the first time, when she went to bed with a man for the whole night, it wasn't because she didn't have a better place to sleep. It was simply because she wanted to be there.

Chapter 8

He got up bright and early and made Birdie her coffee exactly the way he had observed she liked it. Well, hell, last night had been unexpected and amazing. He hadn't thought that would happen. And he hadn't imagined that it could be so . . .

He'd known the sex would be good. Hell, the two of them had enough spark between them to generate a whole forest fire—that much was true. But he hadn't realized he would feel so much. Or that the issues of being her boss and all of that would fall away so easily. But it just didn't matter to their relationship.

Because she was Birdie. Because he had shared so much of himself, and they really were more like friends than boss and employee.

Friends.

He mused on that as he poured his own coffee.

He'd never had sex with a friend before.

But maybe that was what the sex had been missing.

He'd never had an emotional connection to a person he'd been with. Maybe that was why it had never been this good.

He'd meant what he'd said to her too. They could walk with each other for a little while. Hand in hand. It could be nice.

And why not?

Except, it was far too easy to imagine walking along together for many, many years. Watching that copper hair turn silver.

He felt lanced with emotion then.

His father hadn't gotten that with his mother.

He had never seen anyone get that in his family.

What made him think he would?

He wanted it though, so much in that moment that it stilled his breath.

"Lord Almighty," he said.

"Are you praying or summoning me?" came the impish voice behind him. He turned and came face-to-face with his favorite troublemaker of all. Birdie.

"Good morning. I made your coffee. Exactly how you like it."

"How do you know how I like it?"

"I've been watching very carefully." He passed the cup over to her.

"Be careful. A girl could get used to this, and then you might end up with a permanent roommate."

Her eyes caught his and held for a little bit too long. And he realized that the idea of Birdie being his permanent roommate really didn't bother him.

He had never imagined sharing his life with another person.

Not the way she made him think he might want to.

"I'll keep that in mind," he said.

They drove the truck out to the back pasture again. Birdie didn't need instruction at this point. She also didn't complain.

They both worked until they were sweaty, and then he suggested they take a lunch break.

"You feed me so much," she said.

She looked happier. A little more filled out in her cheeks

than when she had first come to work for him. She looked beautiful either way. Always.

When he thought about how much he had disliked her when they were younger, he began to wonder if it had something to do with how carefree she had seemed. How good she was at covering herself in her own sunshine, and doing what felt fun and not necessarily what she was bound to do by duty.

He couldn't understand that. He had always felt burdened.

That cemetery had always loomed large.

She got a wicked little glint in her eye right then, as if she knew the kind of thing he was thinking about. Her mischief.

"We should go eat down by the swimming hole."

"If you want," he said.

"It's just through that thicket, isn't it? Because I do remember sneaking onto your property a few times when I was a kid."

"You know exactly where it is, because I chased you out of there."

"Well, why don't you chase me in there."

He was about to protest, because he had all the food, but Birdie took off like greased lightning, and he could only run after her.

By the time he got through the thicket of trees to the shore of the swimming hole, he was out of breath, and . . . laughing. He couldn't remember the last time he'd laughed like that.

"You almost caught me," she said.

He held the bag up. "I was the keeper of the sandwiches."

"It's fine. Not everybody has the killer instinct to do what needs to be done. Sometimes sacrifices have to be made."

"I'm never sacrificing my sandwich."

She laughed. "You are such a serious man, Gunnar Parsons."

"Less so with you around," he said.

She sat down on a bulging tree root and reached up a hand.

He gave her a sandwich, and then placed a cola in her other outstretched paw.

She grinned. He leaned against the tree to eat, watching her the whole time.

And he had the vague, unhappy realization that this wasn't how things would always be.

She wouldn't always be here. Things would go back to normal. A life where he came home to an empty house, and didn't have anyone to share his deep, terrible thoughts with. Didn't have anyone to help him find light, not-so-terrible thoughts. He finished his sandwich, and it didn't feel satisfying.

When he looked at Birdie again, she was swallowing the remains of her cola. Then she set the can against the tree root and stood up. She looked over at the water, and then she looked back at him.

And with one mischievous grin, she stripped her top off and unhooked her bra, throwing both onto the ground.

He could only watch. Then she stripped the rest of her clothes off and took a running jump off the shoreline, straight into the swimming hole.

"Oh no," she said. "Here I am, skinny-dipping on Parsons land. What are you going to do about it?"

"Birdie . . ."

"Gunnar," she said, mocking his warning tone.

He took a step toward the shoreline.

"Take your clothes off, cowboy. Join me."

"I don't skinny-dip."

"You don't? Looking like that, it's a crime you ever put clothes on at all."

The compliment stunned him. "I . . . well. That's a kind thing to say."

"A kind thing to say," she said, laughing. "As if I'm talking about the weather and not—Come on, Gunnar. Live a little bit. Before you make your way up to that cemetery, maybe you should live a little bit."

He took a sharp breath and stripped his shirt off over his head. Then he undressed, and before he could think it through, jumped straight into the cold water.

When he resurfaced, Birdie was howling with laughter. "Yes!" She threw her arms up, and he caught a glimpse of her breasts just above the surface of the water. "I did it. I was a bad influence on Gunnar Parsons."

"Come here," he said, swimming toward her.

She yelped and disappeared beneath the surface of the water like a siren.

That's what this was. Some kind of witchcraft. Something had grabbed hold of a deep part of himself and changed him. As effective as a spell. Because it couldn't just be real life. What else but magic felt like this? What else could do this to a man?

She resurfaced a moment later and rolled onto her back. The vision that she made like that took his breath away. Her coppery hair floated around her, and he was reminded of a painting he'd seen one time.

"I wish I had a bouquet of lilies," she said solemnly, as she pressed her hands over her breasts. "I'm like the Lady of Shalott, floating away in my untimely, watery demise."

"All right. That's where I've seen it." Some classical painting. And he vaguely remembered the poem.

"Do I look like that? Like a tragic, doomed maiden?"

"Do you want to?"

She went upright, treading water. "I did used to pretend I was."

"Do you like stories like that?"

"Oh yeah. I mean, I was never any good at school, but I really liked reading. I love Greek myths, and Arthurian legends. I really like those old stories, because people are flawed. And who's really a good guy, after all? Not the gods, but often not people either. Plus, the tragedy is so dramatic."

"I never did much like reading. I was more a numbers guy."

"Ooh. Math. No wonder I felt wary of you from the jump."

"I like to hear you talk about stories though," he said.

"Well, I'm glad that when you looked at me, you knew what I felt I looked like." Then she laughed. "That's very silly. I used to pretend in these woods all the time. Yeah, sorry. I sneaked onto your family land more often than you knew. But I wanted to be somewhere else. I loved *The Boxcar Children*, because the kids were on their own, living out in the woods, harvesting blueberries and keeping milk cold in the river. I loved *Anne of Green Gables*, because she was an orphan . . . And I used to dream about becoming an orphan and going to Prince Edward Island because it seemed nicer than here. I liked *The True Confessions of Charlotte Doyle*. Because she befriended the crew on her ship's passage to America and became a pirate. I just loved the idea that I could strike out on my own to become something different. A tragic, romantic figure, maybe." She sighed heavily. "But I'm just Birdie."

He didn't know what he would've thought that meant a couple of weeks ago. But he was stunned by the idea that she could be just anything.

She was filled with dreams. Such a small person who was overflowing with hope, even if she didn't see it that way.

"You mean the toughest, bravest, most miraculous woman I've ever met?"

Her eyes filled with tears. "I didn't mean that, actually."

He could see it. She was gearing up to swim away from him, or maybe even start a fight. Anything other than cry, and he decided that he was going to cut her off at the pass this time. So he closed the distance between them and pulled her into his arms, her body wet and slick against his. And he took her chin in his hand and kissed her.

"Amazing," he whispered, rubbing his lips over hers.

She trembled, and he began to take the kiss deeper.

He knew she thought he was kind of a stick-in-the-mud, but

he knew when passion was appropriate. He knew how to touch a woman. But everything was heightened with her. Better.

He knew exactly what to do for her.

He took her in his arms and swam them both to the shore, carried her to a patch of grass and laid her down in it before going and fetching his jeans and wallet.

Then he kissed her, deep and long.

But it wasn't enough to just kiss her. He wanted to give her every good thing she had been denied in life. He wanted . . .

He kissed her throat, her breasts. He had done all this last night, and it still wasn't enough. He traced the same path—she had said no man had ever done this for her before, but how was that even possible? So he did it. He pleasured her again and again. Until she was crying out his name.

And then he took out the condom, and she put her hand over his.

"Shouldn't I return the favor?"

"You can. Someday. But I don't need you to pay me back. This isn't a transaction."

Her eyes filled with tears again, and he tore the condom open, rolled it onto his length and pressed her back down into the grass.

He kissed her, kissed away the tears that were rolling down her cheeks.

Oh, Birdie. Beautiful, glorious Birdie. Maybe she wouldn't fly away if he made her a nest. Maybe if he became the tree branch. The tree. The mountain that it grew out of. Maybe if he found a way to become a part of her ecosystem, she would stay with him.

And yeah, that scared the hell out of him. It really did.

But as he thrust into her body and kissed her lips, he knew what he wanted. More than ever. More than anything.

He loved Birdie. She was the piece of him that had always been missing. The wild unknown that had never been part of him.

He could be her safety.

They could be with each other. They could share all this delight.

He could give her a wide, warm bed and the same kind of coffee every day. She could make him laugh.

He could tell her the most messed up things about his childhood, and she wouldn't even blink. And he would rail against the unfairness in hers.

They completed each other.

As sure as the sky was blue.

But then he couldn't think, because he was inside her. And he loved her, and that made it like the first time, like the first person.

Different from anything else, and perfect because it was out here.

At this watering hole where he'd once chased her away.

The one thing he needed.

Had that been on purpose? Had he known even then that the scariest, best, biggest thing ever to come into his life would be Birdie Lennox? Had he acted out of instinct because he'd wanted to keep himself safe?

Birdie wasn't about safety.

She was about living. About wild joy.

She was everything.

He touched her between her legs, in time with his thrusts, and she cried out. Only then did he take his own pleasure.

And then he held her. Listening to the sound of the water, the sound of the breeze through the trees.

He wanted to keep her. He didn't know how to say that quite right. He decided not to say anything today. He wanted to take her home one more time, sleep in the same bed, sleep in his house.

He wanted her to really understand what he was offering.

Gunnar Parsons hadn't ever wanted forever; it had always seemed like a dangerous thing.

But he could also see the way his dad had lived unhealed. He would always miss his dad. Would always be grateful for everything his old man had done for him. But he didn't need to pattern his life after his father's. He wanted to live. He wanted to feel things. As Birdie said, he ought to before he ended up in that graveyard. Because that was where he would go, inevitably. Whether he lived or not. Whether he loved or not.

He was choosing love.

Chapter 9

Birdie felt as if she was floating on a dream. It was the strangest thing. Whenever she woke up in Gunnar's arms, she was shocked and delighted. When they went downstairs together and had breakfast together, then showered together, it all seemed . . .

You're playing house.

She didn't like that mean little thought. But it was true. The past few weeks, they'd been playing house. And she was allowing it. She was giving significance to this stop on the winding path she knew she had to take. That scared her a little bit.

Hell, it scared her a lot.

When they sat down to coffee that morning, and he looked at her with intent, she had that thought firmly in her mind: This was playing. Which was why his words shocked her into silence.

"Birdie, I've been thinking. I want you to stay with me."

"Um."

"Great. Very definitive response."

"Well, what do you mean?"

"I guess I ought to back up. I love you."

No one had ever told Birdie Lennox that they loved her. Not her mother, not her father, not any of the men she'd called her lovers. She didn't know how to react to those words being blurted out over a cup of coffee and some scrambled eggs. As matter-of-fact as: *Would you pass the ketchup?* Except it wasn't like that, because it was digging into a soft, vulnerable spot inside her, and she didn't like it.

"You don't mean that," she said.

"I do. I love you. You're my ecosystem, Birdie. I don't know how I'm going to live without you."

"No," she said. "That's not . . . That can't be real. I'm not anybody's *anything.* You're just sex addled."

"I'm not a virgin. As stuffy and uptight as you seem to find me, do you have any complaints about my skills?"

"No," she huffed.

"I didn't get them from nowhere."

That made her face feel hot. Because she didn't like the idea that she was benefiting from things he had learned with other women. She was possessive of him, and she had no right to be.

"I can see that makes you mad," he said. "But it's important that I'm clear here. I'm not in a sex haze. I've never felt this way about anybody before. When I think about you leaving, when I think about my life, my home, my heart going back to the way it was before you tried to steal Pegasus. See, even the horse is Pegasus now, because you've changed everything. You've changed what I thought I could have, what I thought I could be."

"No. That's not possible. Because I told you. I have to fly away."

"But what if you didn't?"

He was looking at her with those earnest blue eyes, and then he got out of his chair and went to his knees in front of her and took her hands in his. "What if you didn't? What if instead, I made you a home here. And you didn't have to leave. What if this place could be yours. I could be yours. You could be mine. You would belong to me, and I would take care of you. And I belong to you, and you'd make me laugh. That's what I want."

"But it can't be that simple."

"Why not?"

"Because it's not how life is. Why did I spend all this time fighting to have a roof over my head or even a shred of human decency from someone when you were just right here, next door, waiting to love me?" She stared at him, and a bubble of hysteria rose up in her chest. "Is that it? You here the whole time just waiting? Then why didn't you come and get me?"

"Because I didn't know. But I do now. I know now that you're mine. I need you. I think that is why I chased you off all those years ago. Because somehow I knew. You were the one for me, and I couldn't handle it then. I had to change. You changed me. Our time together changed me."

"What about me? I haven't changed. I'm just . . . me. And I'm not special, I'm not good." Panic clawed at her. "I'm not good enough for you."

"That's nonsense. You're as good a woman as I've ever known."

"That's not true. I'm a thief and a liar, and you know that."

"Yes, I do know that. I know that you've done those things. I know that you did what you had to do to survive, and I respect it. Because I'm not my dad. I know you. I've listened to you. So don't worry about whether or not you're good enough for me. The only thing I want to know is: do you love me?"

Birdie wanted to run. Did she love him? The very idea terrified her.

"I have to go."

She got up from the table, and she ran out the door. Tears were falling down her cheeks. Oh, how she despised them. She didn't cry. She wasn't weak.

She needed to get away from him. She didn't want him to see.

But her tears were blinding her, and her chest ached. She was running away from the only thing she had ever wanted. She tripped and fell and landed in the gravel, and she sobbed, because it wasn't fair. It wasn't fair, because this was too good to be true. Because men like Gunnar didn't want women like her. Of course she loved him. She had never in all her life loved anyone. And of course she loved him.

She felt strong hands on her arms, and he picked her up from where she had fallen. She looked up into his eyes, so startling and blue. In them she saw a hope and a future she had never let herself dream of.

"Please don't run away from me."

"But I'm afraid. I was never afraid of being hurt. I was never afraid of bad things, because I knew how to fight them. But I don't know how to let somebody love me. And I really don't know how to love anyone back. What if I lose you? What if I disappoint you?"

"You couldn't. I don't need you to be a certain thing, I'm not looking for someone to fill a role in my life. I want to marry you because I want to keep you with me, but if you don't like the idea of marriage, it doesn't have to be that. I don't have any set dream of what love would look like. I never wanted it until I got to know you. It's not about a wife-shaped hole in my life. It's about you, Birdie." With rough thumbs he wiped her tears away from her cheeks. And she didn't feel ashamed about them. She felt safe.

"I wouldn't know how to be a wife, or to be a mother or . . ."

"But we could. We could try those things. Or we could just be together. Like this. We can have whatever we want. Other people don't get to tell us who we are. That I'm too good, or you're too bad. We get to decide. We'll build our own mountain together, and maybe nobody else will understand. Maybe nobody else would be able to live there, but isn't that the point? We're right for each other."

She thought her heart might burst. They *were* right for each other.

He was right for her.

She was just bad enough for him, and he was just good enough for her.

"Gunnar, I do love you."

She threw her arms around his neck and kissed him.

"Do you think you might marry me?"

"Well, why not? I've been a lot of things, but never once respectable."

"I don't want you to be too respectable. I want you to be you."

Birdie Lennox was no stranger to hard times, and now she could no longer say she was a stranger to love.

Because she had Gunnar. And they had the rest of their lives to live every day better than the one before.

Epilogue

The boxcar down by the river was always occupied these days. When Gunnar had found the old train equipment, he had rushed to get it moved onto the property. Sure, it meant that he and Birdie weren't skinny-dipping down by the swimming hole anymore, so populated was it by their children. But it was worth it.

When he finished up with work for the day, it was his first stop.

"I come bearing green apples," he shouted. The door to the boxcar opened, and his youngest son, Carson, poked his head out.

"You're an adult and we can't trust you," Carson said.

"Now," he said, "I know your mom is in there, and she's also an adult."

And that was when he saw Birdie poke her head through the door. Her freckles were darker than usual because she had spent the whole summer outdoors, gardening, playing with the children, riding Pegasus, who was getting on in years now.

"I am a pirate," she said. "So I don't count."

"There were no pirates in *The Boxcar Children*." He only knew that because he had heard her read those books to the kids.

"You could be a pirate too," she said.

Their daughter, Hallie, also looked out, followed by their oldest son, Lachlan. "Dad?" Hallie said. "A pirate?"

"Yes," he said, smiling at Birdie, who gave him a mischievous smile back. "I can be a pirate. I'm about to board the boxcar."

The kids shrieked, and he ran toward them.

He couldn't remember the last time he wasn't laughing.

Oh, what a difference Birdie Parsons had made.